KATE'S Journal

KATE'S

Journal

BRYCE THUNDER KING

Clovercroft Publishing

Kate's Journal

©2020 by Bryce Thunder King

Published by Clovercroft Publishing, Franklin, Tennessee

Cover and Interior Design by Suzanne Lawing

Edited by Lapiz Digital Services

Printed in the United States of America

978-1-950892-10-5

PROLOGUE

"Stop! Stop! You're hurtin' her!" Kate yelled as she jerked at her daddy's pants leg. "You're hurtin' Momma. Stop! Stop!"

The man's right hand dropped and moved around as if it were searching for something, and then it backhanded Kate squarely in the face sending here scooting across the hardwood floor to the opposite wall ten feet away. Her thin, gangly body bounced off the wall, then fell to the floor in a clump. Her loose, pleated dress settled over her legs and feet in a perfect half circle.

"You're never gonna do that again, are you?" the man shouted, then slammed the woman upright against the wall again and again. "I'm gonna teach you a lesson you'll never forget." Holding her upright with his left hand, he grabbed her face in his right hand and slammed her against the wall headfirst.

She stood motionless for a moment, then slumped to the floor.

He looked down at her. "Sara, I'll be back in two weeks and when I get back, you better be nice," he said, then walked to the kitchen door, opened it, and left the house.

Kate stirred. Slowly she lifted her head and looked at her mother. Seeing her disheveled in a pile on the floor, she crawled slowly to her. "Momma, Momma," she uttered.

Sara didn't move.

"Momma, Momma, please wake up," Kate said, then touched her softly on the arm and moved it as best she could.

Sara moved. She raised her head slowly so that she could look at Kate. Her left eye was red and swollen shut, and her cheeks were scraped and red. Blood oozed from one corner of her mouth. Her right eye opened slightly and floated from one side to the other until it focused on Kate. "Are you okay, honey?" she mumbled.

"I don't know, Momma," Kate said, then tears eased down her face.

"Call Aunt Betty, honey. Tell her to come as quick as she can," Sara muttered, then weakly touched Kate's arm. "Daddy will never do this to us again, honey. I promise."

Kate attempted to stand, but fell to the floor.

"Honey," Sara said, "crawl to the bedroom and get Momma's phone. Just pull it off the table."

Kate crawled slowly to Sara's bedroom, grabbed the covers on the side of the bed, and pulled herself up far enough to grab the phone. She dialed her Aunt Betty's number.

"Hello."

"Aunt Betty, Momma's hurt. Please come as quick as you can."

"Your Momma's hurt? Okay…okay, I'll be there. I'll be there in ten minutes."

Seeing a half-full water bottle on her momma's bedside table, Kate stretched and pulled it down, held it in her right hand and crawled slowly and deliberately back to her momma, scraping her kneecaps on the wooden floor and clanging the bottle against the floor as she progressed. The movement aggravated her bruised, delicate face, and she winced from the pain.

"Momma, I brought you a drink."

"Oh, thank you. When's Aunt Betty coming?"

"She said it would be ten minutes."

Sara attempted to hold the bottle, but her hands slipped to her side.

"I'll hold it for you, Momma," Kate said, then with an extraordinary effort lifted the bottle to Sara's lips. Water came slowly from the bottle and spilled to the floor because Sara had difficulty opening her mouth.

"I'm sorry, honey."

"It's okay, Momma."

"Just come close so I can hold you."

Kate moved closer, and her momma put her hands around her. They rested on the floor until the door burst open.

"Sara…oh, my God! You're going to the hospital! I'm calling the ambulance right now."

"No…no, please Betty. We're okay. We just need to get in bed."

Betty rested her hands on her hips and shook her head. "Okay, we'll do it your way, but I really think you need to go to the hospital."

"Thank you."

"Kate, honey, do you want to sleep with Momma tonight?"

"Uh, huh."

"Okay, let me turn the bed back, and I'll come back and get you."

Betty went to Sara's bedroom, turned down the covers, then returned and carried Kate to bed and laid her down gently. "I'm going to help Momma. We'll be here in just a minute."

"Okay, Aunt Betty. Thank you for helping us."

Betty looked at Kate, nodded, and returned to Sara. She helped her up, and they stumbled to the bed. Sara sat on the side of the bed, then Betty wriggled her into the bed. "I'm going to get ice for your eye, Sara. And, Kate, you'll not be going to school tomorrow. I'll go see the principal, so it'll be okay."

"I won't get into trouble?"

"No, honey, I'll take care of it. Now, you rest with Momma while I get some ice."

Betty went to the kitchen, wrapped ice cubes in the centers of two towels, and returned to the bedroom. "Sara, I'm putting this on your eye for about ten minutes. I'll take it off for about fifteen or twenty minutes, then I'll put it back on. We're going to repeat that all night."

"That's too much for you, and I have to go to work tomorrow."

"You're not going anywhere tomorrow. Now, stay still and let the cold towel do its thing. Kate, you have a towel too, and I'm putting it on your cheek. It'll be cold, but it needs to help your cheek get well. That okay?"

"Yes."

"Now, I'm going to make some chicken noodle soup for you two, and I'll be back in a jiffy." Betty went to the kitchen, prepared two bowls of soup, and took them to the bedroom. "Kate, take a sip of this, sweetheart. It'll make you feel better."

Kate slowly sipped the soup. "Thanks, Aunt Betty."

"Okay, sis, it's your time."

Sara lifted her head slightly and sipped the soup. "It's good," she said, her voice barely audible.

Betty continued to feed Sara and Kate a spoonful at a time until both bowls were empty.

"Aunt Betty, my face is getting cold."

"It's time to take the towels off you and your Momma, sweetheart." She lifted the towels from Sara's eye and Kate's cheek. "They have to go back on in twenty minutes. Okay?"

Kate nodded.

Betty took the towels to the kitchen, emptied the ice, then put the towels in the microwave and set it for five minutes. She then went to the linen closet, got a clean sheet and a towel, walked to the couch, and spread the sheet to make a bed. Then she spread the towel over a cushion to make a pillow. She tiptoed to the couch, got Sara's alarm clock, walked back to the couch, and placed the clock on the end table next to her pillow. "I'm going to use you a lot tonight," she said, looking at the clock, "like every twenty minutes."

During the night, Betty established a routine of placing ice packs on Sara's eye and Kate's cheek for ten minutes and off for twenty minutes. The ice barely melted during the ten-minute interval, so she saved the ice for the next treatment. For every twenty-minute interval, she would set the alarm clock and try to sleep. As the night wore on, she felt more and more exhausted.

The windows behind the couch faced east, and Betty saw sun rays filter through the slats in the blinds. "Finally," she said, and then got up, tidied up in the bathroom, and went to Sara's room. "Well, you fellows look about as good as I feel," she said. "Sweetheart, do you want to go to the bathroom?"

"I've already been," Kate said.

"That's great! How about your momma?"

"I think she would like to go."

"Sara, let's see if we can get you up and get you to the bathroom. Can you put your arm around my neck?"

"I think so," Sara said in a low voice, then lifted her arm ever so slowly and put it around Betty's neck. "I'm better," she whispered.

"Yeah, right. You're going to get even better," Betty said. "Ready? Let's scoot you out of the bed."

Sara scooted her leg over the edge of the bed and onto the floor; then with Betty's arms supporting her, she managed to stand up and shuffle to the bathroom.

When Sara and Kate were back in bed, Betty went to the kitchen, made soft boiled eggs, toast, and jelly, got a quart of orange juice, and returned to the bedroom.

"Aunt Betty, my jaw's sore. I can't eat."

"Honey, you have to. I'll put a small spoonful in your mouth. Just chew tiny little bites until you can swallow, and then we'll wash it down with some orange juice."

"Okay."

When they had finished eating, Betty said, "I'm going to the school. I'll tell the principal Kate has the flu; then I'm going by the restaurant to tell the bitch, Margaret, you have the flu too, Sara. When I get back, we're starting the ice pack routine again, and we're going to get you well. I'll get some vitamin C and vitamin K. That'll help with the bruises."

"I think I'll be able to go to work tomorrow," Sara said.

"We'll see. I'll be back soon."

Betty left the house, made her rounds, and returned. She made ice packs and started the same routine that she had used the prior night, which was Sunday. She followed the same routine Monday, Monday night, and Tuesday...making ice packs, breaking for twenty-minute intervals, and cooking three meals a day. When Tuesday night came, she switched from cold packs to very warm packs. "It's time for the blood to get back in your faces and get you well," she told them.

By Wednesday, Kate was up and helping Betty nurse Sara back to good health. Except for her bruised cheek, she appeared to be her normal self.

"Sweetheart, I think with some makeup, you can go back to school tomorrow. What do you think?"

"I hope the kids won't notice me."

"Well, we'll take a look Thursday after you're made up. If you don't look exactly right, we'll wait another day. How's that?"

"Okay."

On Thursday, Betty concealed the bruise on Kate's face with makeup and Betty took her to school.

Sara was able to get up and take care of herself. She had assumed the duty of applying warm packs to her eye. It had turned from a deep black to light black and a dull yellow. When Betty returned, Sara said, "I don't know what we would have done without you."

"I'm your sister. That's what sisters do. Thank God I had the ability to come and help."

Sara hugged her. "You have to be exhausted. Please go home and get some rest. We can make it now."

"Are you sure you're okay? Is there anything else I can do?"

"You've gone beyond the pale. Thank you so much."

"Okay. I'll pick up Kate from school, and then I'll come by Friday and take her to school and pick her up. By the weekend, you two should be doing fine. Does Ricky come home this weekend?"

"No, not this weekend but the weekend after."

"You're sure you're okay?"

"We're fine."

"I'll check on you when I drop Kate off this afternoon."

"Thank you again. I love you."

"Love you too."

Betty left and Sara dressed to go out. She applied makeup on her eye and face, then looked in the mirror. It'll have to do, she thought.

She left the house and drove to the library. She wanted to research some plants. She didn't want to leave a trail on her computer, nor did she want to leave a trail on the library computer, so she selected a hardback novel with a dust cover; then she waited until no one was in the aisle that had books on plants and selected a book. She hurriedly took the dust cover from the novel and placed it on the book on plants. At a corner table where no one could see what she was reading, she began reading. "Roots from plants of the buttercup family contain Aconite, a deadly poison that is untraceable." The sentence exploded in her brain. "A teaspoon of Aconite will kill a big man," another sentence read. "Causing arrhythmic heart function leading to suffocation; only the sign of asphyxia exists. Touching the leaves without wearing gloves may be deadly, as the poison is absorbed rapidly."

She continued reading until she discovered that a plant of the buttercup family may be found at a farm in Kentucky.

When she finished, she again waited until no one was in the aisle where the book on plants had been shelved, then hurried to the shelf, took off the dust cover, and placed the book where it had originally resided. Next, she returned the hardback novel with a dust cover to its shelf. Once she was safely back in her car, she smiled.

Betty brought Kate home Thursday afternoon, then picked her up Friday and brought her home again Friday night. She wished Sara and Kate a great weekend and left to go home.

On Saturday morning, Sara prepared breakfast for Kate and herself. After they finished eating, Sara said, "Honey, use the bathroom and get your game. We're taking a drive."

"Where to, Momma?"

"We're going up to Kentucky to look at some flowers, sweetheart. I may even buy some."

"So we can have flowers in the house?"

"Maybe."

They left the house and got into the car. Sara drove for two hours. Then they stopped at a fast food restaurant so that she and Kate could use the restroom. She drove for another hour and stopped at a farm that was completely isolated from civilization.

"Momma's going to pick some flowers, honey. You stay in the car and watch me. I'll be over there," she said, pointing in a direction where flowers with yellow blooms grew.

"Okay."

Sara got out, looked in both directions, and then opened the trunk. She pulled out rubber gloves, a shovel, a bucket, and some plastic bags. She then walked to the flowers, dug up several plants, and placed them in the plastic bags, then into the bucket. She looked up and in all directions several times. She worked fast but used great caution with the plants, handling them only with gloves. She finished and returned to the car. "Honey, these flowers are a secret just between you and me. Do you understand?"

"Umm…I think so."

"You must never tell anyone we came to the farm or tell anyone we got flowers? Okay? Not daddy, not school, not the police, not Betty, not anyone."

"Okay."

"Good, sweetie. It's our special secret."

"Honey, you go inside and watch TV. I'll be in shortly."

Kate did as her Momma had told her, and Sara went back to the car, got the bucket of flowers, put them inside the utility room, and locked it. As it was nearing 5:00 p.m., Sara started to prepare their dinner. Afterward, they watched TV and then went to bed.

On Sunday, Sara cooked for all of them, brushed Kate's hair, and selected the clothes she would wear each day of the school week. During the afternoon, they left the house and drove to a store that sold party costumes. Sara bought a Tin Man outfit made with foil. She also bought a pointed foil hat.

Sara drove Kate to school each morning and picked her up each afternoon of the following week except Friday, and she asked Betty to drive her home.

"Tell your momma to call me if she needs anything," Betty said when she opened the car door for Kate.

"Okay, I'll tell her. Thanks for coming to get me."

"You're welcome, sweetheart. I'll see you over the weekend."

Kate walked inside through the kitchen door. "I'm home, Momma," she called out. Getting no response, she walked past the dining room and saw her mother dressed in the Tin Man suit and bent over the table. Sara also wore gloves and had a mask over her mouth and nose. Kate tried the door but it was locked. "Momma," she said softly, but Sara continued working on something on the table.

Finally, Sara wrapped the buttercups she had picked in Kentucky and placed them inside a plastic bag. She placed that bag inside another plastic bag. Next, she took off the hat, the suit, and the gloves, and double bagged them. She washed her hands and came out of the dining room where Kate was waiting.

"Honey, don't touch Momma right now. I have to shower, and then I'll be able to talk with you."

"Are you dirty?"

Sara laughed. "I certainly am!"

Sara showered, dressed, and then met Kate in the living room. "Are you okay, sweetheart?"

"I think so. None of the kids made fun of me today."

"They didn't? That's great! There's something I want to talk with you about. Daddy will be home in about two hours. We're going to have him a fine dinner waiting on the table. We have pot roast with potatoes, onions, and carrots. You know your daddy likes to have a drink of whiskey when he gets home, so we're going to have two of the little glasses he likes full of whiskey so that he can just drink 'em right down. After that, your daddy's going to get really sick. He's going to throw up; he's going to be in really bad pain; he's going to stagger around, and then he's going to fall down. Daddy's not going to hurt us anymore, sweetie. Do you understand?"

"Yes, Momma."

"We're not going to do anything; we're not going to call for an ambulance; we're not going to call anyone just then. Okay?"

"Okay."

"When Daddy's not moving anymore, we're going to take some trash bags to the big dumpster behind the grocery store in the shopping center and throw them away. After that, we'll check on Daddy. If he's not moving anymore, we'll call the police. Do you understand all that?"

"We're going to fix it so Daddy's not here anymore."

"But if anybody asks, we don't know what's wrong with Daddy. Understand?"

"Yes."

"Okay, sweetheart, I'm going to fix dinner. Do you want to watch TV?"

Kate smiled and nodded.

"Okay, I'll join you later or I'll call you to dinner."

"Okay."

Sara went to the dining room, set plates for three, placed freshly ironed napkins beside each plate, and carefully placed a fork on the left side of the plate and a knife on the right side with the cutting edge facing toward the plate. She then put on the rubber gloves and got the two large shot glasses she had filled earlier and set them at the head of the table just in front of the plate. Then she pulled off the gloves, retrieved the plastic bag that held her Tin Man Suit from the closet, placed the gloves in the bag, and put the bag back in the closet. She turned around and admired her work on the table. Then she smiled.

The kitchen door opened. "Dinner ready?" a man's voice boomed.

Sara rushed to the kitchen. "It's all ready, honey. I have your whiskey all poured and waiting for you. How's your week?"

"Like any other friggin' week."

Ricky walked to the dining room and straight to the shots of whiskey. He downed the first in one gulp, then the second. He stood still. Something was telling his brain something was wrong. He began sweating profusely: then he gagged. He attempted to grab his chest or his stomach, but his arms appeared paralyzed. He groaned in a deep, wild outburst…then again. His legs buckled; then his chest and arms crashed against the table, and he tumbled to the floor. He groaned again and again, and then he lay completely paralyzed.

Sara put on another pair of plastic gloves, got the plastic bags from the closet, and placed the shot glasses in one of the bags. Next, she took off the gloves and put them in the bag. She carried the plastic bags to her car, and then walked back inside and checked on Ricky.

Kate seemed to be in a trance, her eyes fixated on the TV, when Sara walked into the living room. "Honey, come on. We have to hurry."

They walked out to the car, got in, and Sara drove to the back of the grocery store at the shopping center. After looking around to make sure no one was watching, she pulled the plastic bags from the car and threw them in the dumpster.

"We're going back home," she told Kate as she got back into the car. "Honey, there are two things I want to teach you so that you can take care of yourself when you get bigger. First, never let a man push you around. Second, always write in your journal important things…like tonight. But never write important things so that other people might peek at your journal and find out something you want to keep secret. Write your journal in code so that only you will know what it means. Do you understand?"

"I think I do, Momma."

"Now, we're going home and will call the police. Daddy's gotten really sick. After the police leave and we're alone, I want to teach you about plants—especially about plants in the buttercup family. Some parts of these plants are very dangerous, but they can be helpful too. You may need the information when you grow up. Is that okay with you?"

"Yes."

Sara drove home, called the police, and asked them to hurry. She told the man on the phone that she thought her husband was having a heart attack. Ten minutes passed, and an officer named Sammie knocked on the door. Sammie was one of Sara's patrons at the restaurant.

"Sammie! Thank God it's you! I think Ricky just had a heart attack. Please come in and check him. I'm too torn up to go look. Please look at him! Tell me it's going to be okay."

"I'll check on him, Sara. You wait right here in the kitchen."

Sammie was gone for only two minutes, and then walked back to the kitchen. "You're right, Sara. Ricky has had a massive heart attack. I'm sorry to tell you, but he's gone."

"Oh, no, no, no. No, Ricky can't be gone. Oh, what am I going to do?" She wailed.

CHAPTER 1

"Happy birthday to you! Happy birthday to you! Happy birthday, dear Kate! Happy birthday to you!" the voices sang.

"And Kate, we're all excited about your acquisition of Sara's Kitchen. Your mother loved this place. It's so sad that her knees gave out," a man said.

"Thank you. I don't know you. What's your name?"

"Mark Simmons. I moved here a year ago, and I've been a patron of Sara's Kitchen since I arrived."

"Well, Mark, and all of you, I love this café. It was my mother's home away from home. As many of you know, I worked here off and on since I was ten years old, but I'm here to stay this time."

Kate was imposing as she stood in front of the receptionist's desk at the front of the restaurant. Her five-foot six-inch, one-hundred-twenty-pound frame fit snugly in a tangerine-colored knee-length dress. Her auburn hair flowed freely to the base of her neck, and natural, loose curls accented her face. Her eyes were green. When the light hit them just right, they sparkled like two diamonds set in emeralds.

After her father died, her mother had petitioned the court to have their last name, McDougall, changed to Sara's maiden name, Patterson. Sometimes Kate would stroll toward the kitchen and say, "KP is on kitchen patrol," then laugh in a deep-throated tone as if she were being naughty.

"Kate, cut your cake," someone yelled.

Kate smiled, revealing her pearl-white teeth, which accented her pale pink complexion. "Well, okay," she said, and then walked to the table that held the cake. "Look at that! The icing forms a picture of the café! How beautiful is that!"

"Gladys did that," a woman said. "Gladys at the bakery."

"Well, she did one beautiful job," Kate said. "I'll cut everyone a piece, and drinks are on the house. Bobbie, you and Sharon please help everyone with a drink." She was addressing two employees who were observing the birthday party. "I have a restaurant!" she yelled.

"Kate's our girl! Kate's our girl!" the party of forty sang out in unison.

Kate smiled from ear to ear.

Everyone had their fill of cake and drink, wished Kate a happy birthday, and left the café…everyone except Mark Simmons.

"Kate, thank you for a great time. I'm so happy I could attend this auspicious occasion."

"And I'm happy you got to come, Mark. It was such a surprise."

"Say, do you like the water? I mean, like boating, canoeing, that sort of thing?"

"I do like the water…boating, canoeing, that sort of thing."

They laughed.

"I have a pontoon boat at the marina. Maybe we can take her out one day—when you're not working, of course."

"Maybe."

"Good!" Mark said. "And, congratulations again for your birthday, the café acquisition, and your move back as a permanent resident of our little town." He then extended his hand to Kate.

She shook his hand. "Well, I suppose I'll see you here at the café."

"You definitely will," Mark said, then left.

Bobbie, a woman aged about sixty years with dyed brown hair, which was telltale because of the deep wrinkles on her forehead and around her eyes, walked over to Kate. "Honey, I think Mark was coming on to ya."

A slight redness colored Kate's cheeks. "Bobbie, shame on you for having such evil thoughts," she said and started to walk away, but she turned and said, "Do you really think he was?"

"Oh, I know he was, honey."

"Huh," Kate said, and then went to her tiny office and worked on the café's records, menus, and customer-frequency records until a few minutes before the dinner hour. Then she rushed into the kitchen to help prepare vegetables, bake chicken, and make rolls and biscuits.

"I'll transfer the orders from the kitchen to the pickup counter," Kate said, addressing Gill, the cook, as he warmed a skillet full of onions.

"Great!" Gill said. A balding man of sixty-four and an ex-Marine, Gill was a widower, and the café was all he had in his life. He let everyone know that he was the master cook, and food dishes coming from his kitchen had been prepared with love and care.

Kate and the crew served one hundred and eighteen customers at the dinner hour. Kate counted receipts to be $1,888—$16 average per customer. That's good, Kate thought. After she and the crew had cleaned up for the night, she said, "Tomorrow's Sunday, you guys. Let's keep the tradition going and close tomorrow. Our customers are mainly business and town people who don't come down here on Sunday. Besides, we all need a break."

Bobbie started clapping to show her approval, and everyone joined her and clapped."

When they finished, Kate said, "And besides, Mom's taking me into Nashville for dinner tomorrow night for my birthday. Of course, I have to drive."

Everyone laughed, and then drifted out of the café one by one for a day off. Kate locked up, got into her car, and drove to the outskirts of town where she had purchased a house two months prior. It had been built in the seventies, one-hundred-twenty-feet long by thirty-feet wide with a long stone front porch with white pillars. It had a red brick façade and a stone walkway from the driveway to the front entrance. The house was situated on a three-acre lot and surrounded with trees, which provided privacy. The back lawn stretched for a distance of one hundred fifty feet to a stand of trees. Every chance Kate got, she would sit on the deck off the kitchen with a cup of green tea in hand, simply stare at the back lawn and the woods, and feel something warm inside. She had a pair of fawns that had adopted her woods for habitat, had seen wild turkeys, a groundhog, squirrels, a rabbit, and a snake—all in her backyard.

Tonight she parked in the driveway, got out, and thought about her mother, who had acquired nearly a million dollars from three dead husbands and two men who paid Sara to get out of the marriage. The biggest percentage of the money had come from life insurance policies that had recorded Sara as the only beneficiary, and because the money was from life insurance, it was not taxable. Another large percentage of the money came from the real estate owned by the husband, which had been left to Sara because it was deeded as joint tenancy with right of survivorship. The real estate had been sold with only minimal tax. The remaining money had come from jewelry and personal property, which Sara had sold except for select pieces of jewelry.

Sara had given Kate two hundred thousand in cash to help with the house, and they escaped the tax man by creating a promissory note with annual payments. When the annual payment was due, Sara forgave the payment, and no one greeted the tax man. They had also transferred ownership of the café in the same manner.

"Hello, birthday girl."

"Hi, Mom. How are you feeling?"

"Like a bull rider at the rodeo who's just been thrown off the bull and got kicked in the ass before he hit the ground."

"That good, huh?"

"What are you up to?"

"Well, since you're taking me out tomorrow night, I thought it might be nice for you to spend the night with me. Besides, there's something I want to discuss with you."

"I smell a man in your life."

"You have a good sense of smell!"

"Mothers know all about their daughters. Don't you know that by now, honey?"

"I've been knowing that for a long time, my dear mother. How long do you need before I pick you up?"

"An hour should do it."

"I'll be there," Kate said, then pulled a remote entry fob from her purse, touched the button, and watched the door roll into a cavity in the wall like a roll-top desk. She walked inside and touched the button again; the door emerged, attached itself to a mechanism in the floor, made a faint click, and locked.

To kill time until she needed to leave, she went into her home office, got her journal and a pen, got comfortable, and began writing.

June 12, 2002

I believe today will prove to be an important milestone in my life. Through diligence and patience, I feel I have reached the pinnacle of the mountain. I simply have to fell some trees and keep the underbrush from imposing on my existence. I feel I have solidified my career for the foreseeable future, and my personal comforts are on the correct trajectory. I may allow an unexpected tree to invade the soil on top of my mountain, but I will always cherish my ability to prune it or even banish it from the mountain.

Today is my birthday, and I'm celebrating by having my mother spend the night with me. Tomorrow night, I'm driving us into town, and mother is buying my dinner. Signing off to go get Mom.

Kate had a glass of wine, freshened up, and drove over to her mother's house. Sara lived in the upscale part of Brentwood. When Kate rang the doorbell, the door flew open, and Sara burst out of the house. "Happy birthday, honey!" Sara hugged Kate. "I have something for you, my dear. Let's go inside."

Once inside, Sara rushed off to another room. Only a few seconds passed before she returned with a small box and a large smile. "It's for you, my daughter…for your birthday."

"Mom, you've done enough already, and besides, I really don't need much."

"Shush. Open it! Open it!"

"Mom! What the…"

"It's six carats, honey. Five seemed so ordinary, so I got six. Do you like it?"

"Like it? A six-carat diamond tennis bracelet? It's magnificent!" Kate said, then hugged her mother.

Sara grinned, her eyes sparkling. "I'm so happy you like it. I'm so grateful that I'm financially able to do things for you."

"Thank you so much, Mom. You're a mother every girl should have. Now, let's go over to my place and relax for the evening."

"I'm all packed. If you'll help me with the big bag, I'll get the other one."

They carried the bags to the car, loaded them, and then Kate drove them to her house. They unloaded the bags and went inside.

"Okay, who is he?" Sara asked right away.

"I'm not sure whether he is there. All I know is that he was at my birthday party, and he invited me…sort of…to go out on his boat."

"And his name?"

"Mark Simmons."

"Mark Simmons. I'll remember that name. You're my daughter, and I have responsibility for you, but I trust you'll handle any transgression upon your character. You must know that when someone falls overboard from a boat and doesn't surface, there's only one story and it's from the person that's still on the boat."

"I learned well under your tutelage, Mother."

Sara smiled.

They had a glass of wine and spent the evening talking about their common love—the café—then retired for the night.

The next morning, Kate dressed, walked to the kitchen, and looked out at the backyard. About a hundred feet from her deck, a deer grazed. She ran to her mother's bedroom. "Mom! Mom!"

"Wha...wha...what...what's wrong?"

"Hurry! Quick! And don't make any noise."

They hurried to the kitchen, and the doe was still grazing.

"Ssshhh. Look, Mom," Kate said, pointing toward the doe.

"Well, I'll be! Honey, you have your own deer," Kate said, talking as quietly as she could.

"Mom, I love it here."

"I'm so happy for you, honey."

They stepped into the kitchen and prepared breakfast. Kate carried everything outside to the deck table, and they ate. Afterward, Kate asked Sara to make a deal with her. "Mom," she said, "I'll clear the table and put everything away if you'll go antique shopping with me."

"I'd love that."

Kate cleared the deck table, then freshened her makeup, changed into a sundress, and went to four antique shops with her mom. They returned home midafternoon and changed clothes, then drove to Germantown.

"I selected a dimly lit, quiet restaurant, honey. If it's okay with you, we'll drink and eat slowly and enjoy the night out. After all, we get to celebrate a birthday only once a year." "Sounds like a wonderful birthday planned for me, Mom. Thank you."

They arrived at the restaurant and spent the next three hours sipping wine, eating a specially prepared dish by the chef at Sara's request, and each enjoying strawberry-colored cake, topped with strawberry frosting, real strawberries, and a small scoop of vanilla ice cream.

After taking her mother home, Kate returned to her own home and wrote in her journal before going to bed.

June 13, 2002

Mom spent the night with me last night. We talked about the café most of the night. Today we saw my dear, went antique shopping, then went to a restaurant in Germantown to celebrate my birthday. The food and atmosphere were wonderful. It was great spending time with Mom…just her and me enjoying each other. I'll sign off. I'm going to bed, and tomorrow is Monday and time to go to enjoy time with the customers.

CHAPTER 2

Kate got up at 5:00 a.m., showered, dressed, and drove to the café, arriving at 6:15 a.m. Because it was summer, it was still daylight; however, she thought about the winter months when it would be dark at the same time in the morning. *Time to go to school, get a permit, and start carrying a shooter,* she thought. It might also be wise to have Bobbie come in with her during the winter months, she decided.

She made coffee, opened the door for the pastry delivery man at 6:45 a.m., steamed two bags of home-style potatoes, scrambled two dozen eggs, and had the potatoes and eggs in the warming oven when Bobbie, Sharon, and Gill reported to work promptly at seven. Three customers followed them, and the morning rush hour began. The next hour and a half flew by in a flurry of activity. Almost half of the customers had to report for work at their respective offices at eight, and nearly all of the remaining customers had to report at 8:30. Several professional people came in for their morning coffee at about 8:15, but they didn't open their offices until nine.

After all the customers had gone to their jobs, and all the tables were cleared and cleaned, and dishes were put in the washer, Kate and the crew took a break and had coffee and a pastry—if any were left. It was at that time every morning that Kate became just one of the crew as everyone talked about what they had done on their day off. Bobbie's husband was disabled, and they seldom ventured away from home, so her statement was about the same every Monday. "We didn't do anything. Hugh just won't budge from the house, so I'm stuck." Then she laughed, and her captivity didn't seem so painful.

Sharon was forty, had brown hair, and was very thin. Her face was long and thin, and she was not particularly attractive. She lived with her parents, having been jilted by a lover when she was twenty-eight and never recovered. She rarely did anything or went anywhere by herself, using the excuse that she had to take care of her parents.

Gill, on the other hand, stayed active. During hunting season, he was in the woods whenever he had free time. When he wasn't in the woods, he was on the lake in his bass boat. He had more stories than Mark Twain's *Huckleberry Finn*, and Bobbie and Sharon derived much pleasure hearing about his adventures. This Monday, he told about accidentally disturbing a hornet's nest when he went into the woods on Sunday. To escape their wrath, he had quickly inflated his tent, crawled inside, and stayed there four hours. Even after that length of time, the hornets still buzzed outside; so he slowly took steps until he was several feet away from the area while holding the tent intact and around him as he moved. When he emerged from the tent, one hornet, having hung on for the ride, came at him like a missile, stung him on the right side of the neck, and then vanished. He spent most of Sunday night making a paste of baking soda and water to plaster on his neck with the belief that it would draw out any infection. Everyone laughed profusely at his misfortune.

"He didn't come in this morning," Bobbie said.

"Who?" Kate asked.

"Mark Simmons."

"Was he supposed to?"

"He comes in every Monday," Bobbie said, "and every Tuesday through Friday. That's his last day of the week, because he doesn't work on Saturday."

"He doesn't?" Kate said, then added, "I really wasn't looking for him."

"He'll be in," Bobbie said.

The days passed, and the same routine was practiced every morning, every lunch hour, and every dinner. Nearly all the customers were the same day after day, and their food preferences were the same day after day. Friday came, and Mark Simmons had not appeared for the entire week. Demands of the day kept Kate busy, and it seemed the day had flown by when the dinner hour started and finished. Kate, with her back to the entrance door, wiped a table vigorously when a voice sounded. "Is it too late to get a cup of coffee?"

Kate turned and looked. "It's you! I mean…no, it's not too late. Let's see, you take yours with cream."

"I do. You looked shocked to see me, or was I just imagining a look?"

Kate seemed occupied with her thoughts for a moment, then said, "No, just a tired look. It's been a tiring week. Have you been in this week?"

"No, I've been on the road this week, and I'm really thirsty."

"Oh, I'm sorry," Kate said and attempted to fake a laugh. "Coffee? Coming up," she said, then poured a cup and handed it to Mark along with a container of cream.

"So, you've had a rough week?"

"Well, a little, I suppose. Five a.m. comes quickly when you don't go to bed until eleven or after."

"Can you take a break on Sunday? I'll fill the pontoon boat up, and we can take a cruise on the lake. The bartender will serve your favorite wine or liquor. To top that, the weather's supposed to be spectacular."

Kate was silent for a moment, then said, "With all those positives, who can say no?"

"Fantastic! Will ten o'clock be ok? I'll pick you up at your house."

Kate was silent again but finally said, "I'll be here at the café. I have some things to do here. Just pick me up here." Then she thought, *Why didn't I just let him pick me up?*

"Okay, that'll work. I'll be here promptly at ten. Have a great Saturday. Say, what do you drink? I mean, wine, liquor…"

"Only wine."

"Cabernet sauvignon, pinot noir, merlot?"

"Let's try merlot."

"I know just the brand. See you Sunday. Oh, I forgot to pay you. This should do it," Mark said and put a five-dollar bill on the counter.

"It's on the house," Kate said, "and besides it's only two-fifty."

"You have to make a profit. Consider it your last tip of the day," he said, and then walked out smiling.

Kate stood still for a moment. Her heart beats a little faster. *I think I just made a date,* she thought.

"We couldn't help but hear," Bobbie said. "Kate has a date, and we want to hear all about it Monday morning."

Kate blushed. "It's just a boat ride."

"We still want to hear," Bobbie said, chuckling.

As soon as the crew had gone home, Kate texted her mother. "There is a he," she typed, "and I've agreed to go on his boat for a ride on Sunday."

"I'm so happy for you, honey. You'll have a great time, and I can't wait to hear about it when you return."

Kate smiled. She closed the café and drove home as quickly as possible without pushing the speed limit too much. She got out of the car and rushed into the house. *What am I going to wear?* she thought. *Why didn't I ask him what he's wearing…shorts or pants? I'm sure not going to call him. I don't even have his number if I wanted to. I'll go by the marina and see what other people wear. No, I can't do that. He may be there and see me. Then he'll want to know what I'm doing there. I'll just have to wait until tomorrow, but the stores will close before I can get out of the café. If I have to buy something, maybe mom can go get whatever it is and bring it to the restaurant or here.*

She prepared for bed and told herself she had to go to sleep, but she tossed and turned for two hours before she went to sleep.

Five o'clock came really early, but she climbed out of the bed and prepared to go to work. She arrived at 6:05, a bit earlier than usual. She made coffee, and the entrance door chimed. Thinking it was the pastry delivery man, she hurried to the door and unlocked it. There stood Mark.

"Good morning. I just stopped to tell you I'm wearing shorts. Is that okay with you?"

Stunned for a moment, she said, "Sure, that's great. I'll just wear shorts too."

"Great! See you tomorrow."

"Okay, tomorrow. Say, do you want coffee?"

"I will. For the road, though. I'm pressed for time today."

"I'll be right back," Kate said, then quickly poured a cup of coffee, put it in a container of cream in a carryout box, and gave it to Mark. They said their goodbyes, and Kate went back to work, smiling.

This man is really polite, she thought. *Shorts! Do I have shorts?* She couldn't think, so she texted her mother. "Help! Need for you to shop for me a pair of shorts today and bring them by the café. Please, no conflict with my hair. Thanks, Mom."

The day dragged on as Kate watched for her mother. Finally, at 2:00 p.m., Sara breezed into the café. "Come and look, honey."

Kate didn't want customers or her staff to see, so she pulled the shorts to the top of the bag and peeked at them. They were white with twisted white pieces of rope tied at the end that hung from the belt loops on each side of the shorts. The ends did not protrude farther than the bottom hem of the shorts, and they added a bit of casual, carefree look to the shorts. A light blue blouse that buttoned just above the valley of the breasts was also in the bag.

"Mom, you did great! I love the shorts and top!"

"I thought they were really spiffy," Sara said.

"They're both spiffy and pretty," Kate said. "They're great with my complexion."

"Call me, honey…tomorrow, when you get home."

"I will. Wish me luck."

"Good luck. Talk with you tomorrow."

Sara left the café, and Kate looked in the bag again and smiled. *Things are working out,* she thought. She finished the day, closed the café, hurried home, and got ready for bed. She set the alarm for 6:00 a.m. *I'll just tie my hair in a pony tail tomorrow,* she thought. *I'll wear white shoes, but take flip-flops in my beach bag just in case. Go to sleep,* she told herself. *Go to sleep.*

She fell asleep at midnight and jumped when the alarm went off. *Time to get up,* she thought. She pulled on her housecoat, went to the kitchen, and made coffee. Before getting in the shower she thought, *Should I eat something first? No, I'll grab a bite at the café. Why am I so disorganized? I need to get a grip.*

After her shower, she worked for thirty minutes getting her hair just right, then put on the clothes her mother had purchased. Then she tried on two other outfits from her closet. Finally, she went back to the white shorts and blue top, checked herself in the mirror, grabbed her bag, looked about the house to make sure everything was in order, and then left for the café.

Kate looked at her watch as she unlocked the door to the café and went inside. It was 9:40 a.m. *I hope no customers saw me,* she thought. *That would foul up the morning. And it's too late for me to eat. My teeth are clean, so I'll do nothing…well, I can't just be waiting. I'll work on the books.*

The hands on the café seemed to be stuck in neutral. Kate attempted to post her deposits for the week while looking up at the door every thirty seconds. *Whatever happens, he can't catch me watching the door,* she thought.

At precisely ten, someone rattled the doorknob. Kate looked up to see whether it is Mark Simmons. She walked at a measured pace so as not to appear overly enthusiastic, then unlocked the door. "Good morning. You're right on time."

"Good morning," Mark said and pretended to tip an imaginary hat as a thank-you gesture. "I'm not obsessed with being on time, but I've noticed that even chronic late people notice that other people are on time, so I make it a point to try to be on time whatever I do, and it becomes a habit…like everything else is a habit. Whew! That was a mouthful. Have you been working?"

"I wish I could say yes, but I was late getting here," Kate said and laughed.

Mark smiled. "You're very brave to tackle the café by yourself. I know, it's a lot of work."

"I have a loyal staff, and that makes a lot of difference."

"Well, if you ever need help with sweeping, mopping, washing dishes, whatever…please call me."

"I'll remember that. Have you noticed that we both have blue tops and white bottoms?"

"I did notice. Perfect outfits for a great day on the water, and there are two hats on the boat, a captain's hat and a first mate's hat, that is, if you wear a hat and you don't mind being the first mate."

"I do wear hats, and the first mate is right up my alley. Do you want coffee?"

"If you have made some, it would be great! But please don't take the trouble if you don't have it made."

"No trouble. I'd sort of like to have a cup myself." Kate walked over to the coffee maker, inserted the package of coffee, and poured water into the reservoir. As she went through the motions, she sized Mark up in her head. He was probably in his early thirties, six feet tall, and maybe a hundred and seventy-five pounds. He had dark eyes, dark hair, slightly tanned face and arms, and rounded facial features that complemented his eyes and hair. He walked authoritatively but was extremely polite and courteous.

"What do you do, Mark…that is, career-wise?"

"I oversee compliance for sixty securities offices in Kentucky, Tennessee, North Carolina, and Georgia. Each office offers a full-service platform for selling and buying securities for clients. So, I travel a lot."

"These offices sell stocks and bonds…that sort of thing?" Kate asked, then poured each of them a cup of coffee, and gave Mark a cup along with cream and sugar.

"Thank you for the coffee. Yes, the offices sell stocks and bonds… that sort of thing," Mark said and smiled.

The repetition of sentences had caught on between the two, and Kate smiled.

"Well, when I get some dollars, you'll have to help me invest," she said with a perky tone.

"It'll be a pleasure, but I don't do the actual investing. I look over the shoulder of the person who's actually doing the investing; then I watch to make sure they're doing the right thing for the client. In your case, I'll steer you to the right person, then watch over their shoulder."

Kate laughed. "All I have to do is get the dollars."

"I believe the dollars will come."

They finished their coffee. Meanwhile, Mark put a ten-dollar bill on the counter.

"No, no, it's on the house."

"Kate, I have an expense account. Please accept it because that's the only sale for the day."

"Since you put it that way, it'll go in the till." With an animated twist of her wrist, she picked up the bill and placed it in front of the cash register.

"Ready to have some fun?" Mark asked.

"Ready."

They left the restaurant and walked toward Mark's vehicle, a Mercedes convertible. "Wow! I'm impressed," Kate said.

Mark grinned "Well, I wanted to impress you, so I brought the

Sunday wheels."

"You've done it. Now, how do I get in?"

Mark helped her in and they took off for the Marina.

"I love it!" Kate said as sun rays danced across the top of her head. The rushing wind would pick up her red hair and toss it from one side to the other, creating a brilliant display of dazzling red as the sun struck different parts of her hair.

He smiled over at her, his hair flying carefree.

They arrived at the slip where the boat was docked, got out, and walked to the boat.

"Here she is, *Flyin Mark*.

"She's beautiful."

"She's outfitted with a sound system, bathroom, and kitchen. Shall we?"

They boarded the boat. Mark started the engine and backed slowly away from the slip. Once they were underway, he steered toward the middle of the lake; houses near the lake became smaller and smaller. They cruised for two hours, and then docked on a small island. The island was a quarter-mile wide and boasted an abundance of tall pine trees. They walked the width of it, found a rock formation that overlooked the lake, and had lunch. Afterward, they returned to the boat and listened to music for an hour as the water lapped against the hull. Later, they explored the shoreline for two hours before heading back to the slip.

On the drive back to town, Kate glowed. That was the most relaxing, most beautiful day I've had in a long, long time," she said.

"Everything was perfect, wasn't it?" Mark said. "The lake was beautiful, the island was fun to explore, the lunch was great…the company was wonderful…a magical day."

"And I agree with all you said."

As Mark pulled up to the restaurant and parked, he asked Kate if she liked the band Chicago.

"I love Chicago."

"They're playing next Saturday night at eight o'clock at the amphitheater. Would you like to go...that is, if work permits?"

"I think I can work it out. Leave here at seven?"

"Seven would be great. There's a parking lot across the street from the theater. I'm out of town next week, so I won't be in for breakfast until Saturday morning."

"Have a safe trip," Kate said, then got out of the car, thanked Mark again and headed home.

In her journal, she jotted down only a few notes before switching off the bedside lamp.

June 20, 2002

Today I was on the lake in a pontoon boat with M/S, who continues to amaze me. He is still polite; he is still courteous; he is still thoughtful; he has become Mr. Wonderful. I believe sincerely there are good things coming from this relationship. I believe my mother's teachings will not be necessary in the present case...and, I'm happy about that. Although a magical day, I am tired, but I must go see my mother.

Signing off.

CHAPTER 3

"Good morning, Miss Kate. It's Saturday," Bobbie said, her voice high-pitched as if she were making an announcement. "Have you heard from him?"

Kate put her hand on Bobbie's shoulder. "He's called every morning," she said. "Monday, to tell me he enjoyed our outing on the lake; Tuesday, to ask me how my first day back at work went; Wednesday, to remind me it was hump day and to have a good day; Thursday, just to say 'hello'; Friday, to confirm that we're going to see *Chicago*; this morning, to say that he would see me for breakfast…and I can't wait."

"Honey, we're all so happy for you," Bobbie said.

Kate embraced her. "Thanks, and don't worry…if anything were to happen, you know…down the road, I'll never sell the café. Everyone has a job for as long as they want."

Bobbie grinned. "We all appreciate that."

Mark came for breakfast promptly at seven. Kate talked with him for five minutes, but the morning crowd kept her busy, so she told him she would see him at seven that night.

It was extremely busy for Saturday, and it was six o'clock before Kate knew it. She had brought a change of clothes for the Chicago show, so she slipped into the employees' restroom and changed clothes. She finished dressing and freshening her face and hair at six fifty-eight, and then walked to the dining area of the café. Sure enough, Mark walked in at exactly seven o'clock.

"You're a master at the time, mister," Kate said.

Mark smiled. "You're too kind, and you look stunning."

"Thank you. Are we ready to go rock and roll?"

"We are. Good night, Bobbie. Good night, Sharon," Mark said as they left.

Mark drove into town and to the parking area and found a parking spot near the street. "It's our lucky night," he said. "We'll be able to get out before the traffic gets so heavy."

"That's a plan. How was your week?" Kate asked as Mark opened the door for her to get out of the car.

"I flew to Atlanta; I flew to Charlotte; I flew to Lexington; I flew, flew, flew. I had strange pillows; I had strange beds; I had strange people everywhere. It was fun at first…traveling, but it's getting to be a real chore."

"Sorry, it does sound awful."

They walked across the street and into the theater and found their seats. The place was busy as a beehive. They amused themselves by watching people as they came in, left, or milled around. Some didn't seem to know what to do or where to go. Thirty minutes later, the show began. When the song, *Wishing You Were Here*, was sung, Mark put his arm around Kate's shoulder and kissed her lightly on the cheek. Kate turned to look at him, but he didn't look her way.

After the show, Mark drove back to the café, then walked Kate to her car. They embraced and kissed but only in a tepid way.

"Good night, beautiful lady. Do you have time for dinner tomorrow night?"

"I do, and thank you for a wonderful evening. It was a great show."

"I thought the show was fabulous, and I was elated just being with you."

She smiled. "Good night."

"Night."

Kate drove home, went inside, and immediately retrieved her journal. She wrote:

June 26, 2002

I went with M/S to see the band, Chicago, tonight, and it was a great show. M/S kissed me on the cheek during the show, and I wanted a more intimate kiss, but it was not to be. He kissed me briefly when he let me off at the café after the show, but it still was not enough. Sometimes, I feel that he doesn't want to make a commitment, and he purposely doesn't lead me on. I already have strong feelings for him, but I am going to have to perform a lot more analysis of our relationship. I'm tired tonight, so I'm turning in. Mark is taking me to dinner tomorrow night.

During the next eight weeks, Mark and Kate did something every Sunday…canoeing, hiking, theater in Atlanta, antique shopping, picnicking, a concert, and two outings on the pontoon boat. Kate thought about Mark a lot when they were not together. She knew her heart had grown an attachment to him, so she maintained good thoughts about him although she asked herself over and over about their intimacy. In all their outings, he had not demonstrated a deep affection for her nor had he ever suggested they become sexually active.

On August 27, he called. "Do you have a passport?" he asked.

"No, should I?"

"Would you like to go on a cruise? It would sail on September 13 and return on the seventeenth. We would fly to Miami, and board the ship at the Port of Miami. We would dock at four different ports in the Caribbean, so we could shop and sightsee to our heart's content."

"I've never been on a cruise, but I've always wanted to…well, yes, I'd love to go. What do I do? Get a passport?"

"Yes, but you'll have to get it expedited because we only have about seventeen days."

"I get it at the post office, right?"

"Yes, the main post office."

"I know the people there. I'm sure I can pull it off. What about clothes? I mean, the weather. What kind of clothes do we wear for the weather?"

"It's a standard eighty-five degree wherever you go. You'll need shorts, casual wear, and one dress-up outfit for the captain's night."

"Done. I'll get on it as soon as we hang up."

"I'll be in touch, and I'll make a list of things to take and the places we'll being visiting."

"Great!"

Kate turned to see Bobbie. "I'm going on a cruise!" she said, beaming from ear to ear.

"You and Mark?"

"Yes."

"Oh, honey, I don't have words to tell you how happy I am for you."

"I have to get a passport. Can you hold the fort while I go to the post office and apply for it?"

"Oh, sure, honey."

Kate rushed to her car and, as if an afterthought, called her mother. "Mom, I've been invited to go on a cruise."

"You have?"

"Yes, but that leaves the café…"

"It's wonderful you get to go, and don't worry, honey, I'll sub for you. When should I report for duty?"

"September 13."

"I'll be there."

"Oh, Mom, thank you so much. I love you."

"I love you too."

At the post office, Kate applied for a passport. She told the manager her urgency in securing one and was advised that she should have it in her hands in seven days. Breathing a sigh of relief, Kate left the office and returned to the café. The demands of the business drew her into it, and she stayed busy, trip or no trip. During the breaks that came in mid-morning and mid-afternoon, she researched the weather in the Caribbean Islands and what women wore on cruise ships. Even though customers demanded her attention, she thought about getting ready for the cruise.

As if it were attached to a whirlwind, September 13 came, and Mark and Kate were in the air to Miami. They arrived and took a cab to the port and gazed at their ship.

"That is one huge ship," Kate said. "It must be three or four football fields long and two football fields tall."

Mark laughed. "It's one huge floating vessel," he said. "Let's go and board her."

They got in line to present their passports and credentials to the ship and port representative. After much waiting, they were cleared to board.

They walked up the gangplank to the ship and found their suite on the fourteenth deck, which turned out to be a top-of-the-line suite featuring a bedroom with two beds, a sitting room, floor-to-ceiling windows, two bathrooms, a balcony, and access to a private restaurant.

"This is wonderful," Kate gushed, then rushed to the balcony.

"Come, come, look at this view," she said, waving for Mark to follow her.

He followed, then put his hand around her waist, and pulled her close beside him. "This is going to be a wonderful adventure," he said.

"This is just marvelous. Thank you for inviting me to come and witness this wonderful adventure."

"Just you and me and a little piece of heaven."

"Those people on the dock…they're loading the ship?"

"Supplies and food. Takes a lot of stuff to feed, entertain, and service four thousand passengers and half as many crews."

"Wow!"

They watched as the ship's personnel moved a mountain of food and supplies from the dock to the ship, but as soon as the last pallet left the dock and was moved to the ship, they were underway. The ship moved from the dock, down a long inlet flanked by houses that faced the water, and cranes that loaded and offloaded goods, machinery, and equipment from the ships that used the Port of Miami. Twenty minutes later, they cleared the inlet and sailed into the Atlantic Ocean.

Kate held her hands to her mouth. "Oh, my God! How beautiful! Water everywhere, farther than the eye can see."

Mark smiled. "When mankind and womankind run out of land, they can move here on the water; you sure could put a lot of house-boats out here."

Kate laughed. "Might be a little rocky, if you watch how rough the water is."

"It would be rocky," he agreed.

An announcement soon came on the ship's announcement sys-tem requesting all passengers assemble on the deck for a muster drill. Mark and Kate took their lifejackets and joined other passengers on the deck. Ship personnel directed them to form a line; then they were advised of their designated area and the lifeboat they would board in the event of a catastrophe. Following the short drill, passengers were free to return to their quarters or do whatever they wished.

During the drill, Kate was preoccupied with the agenda for the eve-ning and night. There were two beds. Would they share one bed or would Mark suggest they sleep in separate beds?

"Shall we go exploring?" Mark asked.

"Let's do it."

They started on the top deck, viewed the swimming pool, aqua park, mini-golf course, and much more. Then they took the elevator to Deck 5, then to Deck 6, and visited the casino, different theaters, library, bars, and a simulated city street with several shops called City Street. A parade with a multi-instrument band and singers grabbed the attention of everyone as they marched down the street playing and singing.

"If you didn't know better, you would think this is Times Square in New York," Mark said loudly, trying to make himself heard above the parade noise.

"You would!" Kate said, excited. "Isn't this just beautiful? It's like we're in a real city."

Mark smiled. "You're having a great time, aren't you?"

"I am, and you're to blame."

"It's so warming to see you so happy."

They spent the afternoon discovering one area of interest after another, then dressed and went to the private steakhouse for dinner at six. It was situated in one corner of the ship enclosed with windows from the deck to the ceiling, and it created a stunning view of the ocean.

"This should be a real treat," Kate said. She reached for his hand and held it in hers. "Thank you," she said, her voice so soft that it was barely above a whisper.

They had an extended dinner and did not leave the restaurant until eight o'clock.

"That was the best meal, the best service, the most attention I've ever experienced," Kate said.

"I agree. We had it all. You couldn't imagine anything to ask for because it was all there…the delicious food, the impeccable service, and just the right measure of attention. Do you want to take a stroll… maybe a cup of coffee later?"

"I'd love it."

They took the elevator to Deck 6 where City Street was situated and were amazed at the activities going on. They sang along with the singers, danced, watched a clown show, and then settled down for a cup of coffee at a café.

After they finished their coffee, Mark said, "It's ten-thirty. Do you want to settle in for the night?"

"Let's. It's been a very long day."

They returned to their suite, walked inside, and Mark said,

"Sweetheart, I need to go make arrangements for our special night with the captain. Do you mind if I leave you alone?"

"No, no, go ahead. I'll occupy myself with a movie."

"I may be gone for an hour. Will you be okay?"

"Oh, sure. Do whatever you need to do. I'll be perfectly okay."

Mark kissed her quickly on the cheek and walked out of the suite. Kate looked at herself in the mirror and said, "A date with the captain...now, that'll be special." She turned on the TV, went into the dressing room, and changed into a nightgown and robe. Then she went to the bathroom, brushed her teeth, and walked to the space that separated the two beds. "Do I take you, or do I take you?" she asked, pointing to one bed and then the other. "I'll take you," she said, and pulled the covers back on the bed to the right. Then she climbed in and pulled the covers over her.

Minutes passed, then an hour, and Kate fell asleep and did not wake up until the next morning. She jumped with a start.

"Good morning," Mark said from the second bed. "You were sleeping so soundly when I returned last night I couldn't bring myself to wake you."

"Oh, I did sleep soundly. I don't remember what time I fell asleep."

"I wasn't gone too long, so you must have fallen asleep as soon as I left."

"I guess. Did you get the captain squared away?"

"Funny you ask. After I'd waited for at least forty-five minutes and was just about to be granted entrance to his office, he had an emergency on the bridge and rushed away. His aide asked me to return tonight after all the ship responsibilities had been met. He suggested about ten o'clock."

"Well, maybe you'll be successful this time around," Kate said, and quickly pulled on her knee-length white cotton robe over her red, silk pajamas. She had brought a short, sexy, chiffon robe, but she wasn't in the mood to put it on. "Are we having breakfast?"

"Absolutely. We qualify to have breakfast at the restaurant, so we don't have to go down and get pushed around by the crowd at the buffet."

"Do I have time to take a shower?"

"You do, and I'll be taking mine."

I'm on a cruise, and my date is gone for two nights in a row, Kate thought. *This is not what I expected, not what I dreamed of.*

Kate brushed her teeth and took a shower, then dressed in the bathroom. She looked at herself in the mirror and slowly put on makeup. She used as much time as she could because she wasn't about to leave the bathroom before Mark was ready. Finally, she thought she should go out to the sitting room.

"Well, you look great! Ready for Day 2 on the ship?"

"Breakfast first?"

"Of course. I believe we dock in Antigua tomorrow morning. The island has wonderful shopping, beautiful beaches, gambling. The ship has more excursions than you can imagine. What's your preference?"

"Let's do some shopping, look at the excursion choices."

"Done. I'll go by tonight and get a booklet from the excursions desk."

They went to the private restaurant and had breakfast, then went to the top deck, played tennis and mini-golf, and tried rock climbing. When they were tired of playing, they had a hot dog and potato chips for lunch topped off with a giant soft serve ice cream cone.

Later, they took the elevator to Deck 6 and spent time in the library.

"Do you want to try your hand with the slot machines?" Mark asked.

"Let's try them. We might break the bank." Kate laughed.

They played in the casino for two hours, then went back to their suite, freshened up, and had dinner.

"Want to go down to City Street and see what's going on?" Mark asked.

"Sure. Maybe they'll have another parade going on."

They walked to City Street and were again amazed at the activity.

"This place never slows down," Mark said.

"This is where the action is," Kate said. "Look at those people on stilts."

"Looks like Mardi Gras."

Like the night before, they returned to their suite at a quarter to ten, then Mark left to see the captain.

Kate went to the bathroom, put on her pajamas, brushed her teeth, took off her makeup, then walked to her bed and climbed in. She turned on the TV but soon fell asleep.

The next morning, she awakened, put on her robe, and saw Mark on the balcony with a cup of coffee. She walked out and met him.

"Well, good morning! I brought a coffee for you if you want."

"I have to brush my teeth first, but I'll be back. Maybe that'll wake me."

She brushed her teeth and walked back to the balcony. "How'd it go last night...with the captain?"

"It went great. We're having dinner at the captain's table, but I suggested an additional activity for us, which the captain is going to consider. If it's okay with you, I'll go back tonight and work out the details."

Kate studied his eyes and facial features for a moment, then said, "Oh, sure it's okay. Ten o'clock is about my curfew anyway."

"Good. Oh, we're getting ready to dock. I researched some spots to visit on the island. One is a vacated sugar plantation run by the British when they had control of the island; another is Nelson's Dockyard National Park and Museum. A third is Shirley Heights, which overlooks the island and is said to have a magnificent view."

"What about shopping?"

"Of course, shopping. We should be docking at St. John's, which is the capital and is said to have wonderful items we'll be interested in."

"What time do we get off the ship?"

"Nine."

"Should we have a bite to eat before we get off?"

"Let's do. I'll wait out here until you get ready."

"I'll be about forty-five minutes."

"Take as much time as you want."

Kate went inside the suite to the bathroom that she had been using and took a quick shower. She pulled her hair into a ponytail, rubbed lotion on her face and hands, and dressed in white capris, a lavender V-neck top, and leather sandals.

"You look better with each different change," Mark said when Kate walked toward him.

"Thank you."

They ate breakfast, took the elevator to Deck 7, then took the gangway to exit the ship and stepped onto the dock. They walked away from the ship and stopped.

"We join that group that's holding number three sign," Mark said.

Kate turned her head, looking left then right, taking in all the scenery; then she said, "Number three. Right."

They spent the morning seeing all the points of interest Mark had suggested, then had lunch at an outdoor restaurant in St. John's. Later, they walked through the shops, and Kate bought a pearl necklace for her mother, bracelets for Bobbie and Sharon, and a leather wallet for Gill. Mark bought several rum cakes for business associates and had them shipped to his home address. Then they returned to the ship, had dinner, and returned to their suite.

"Let's look at St. John's at night," Kate said, motioning for Mark to follow her to the balcony.

Mark joined here, looked at the lights for a moment, then said, "If it's okay with you, I'll go complete the details for the activities."

Kate hesitated for a moment and pretended to be consumed with the scenery, then jerked her head as if returning to reality, and said, "Oh, sure. Go ahead. I'm going to enjoy the scenery."

"Okay, I'll be back as soon as possible."

"Okay."

Mark left the suite. As soon as the door closed, Kate ran through the suite, grabbed the entrance key to the suite, and eased the entrance door open. She looked down the hall and spotted Mark as he walked to the elevator and reminded herself that he was wearing multicolored, silk shirt, untucked from his light blue walking shorts, so it blew from side to side as he walked. She hurried to get closer to him before he reached the elevator, then hid behind one of the service carts parked along the walkway.

Suddenly, Mark disappeared into an elevator on the left. She ran to the elevator and watched as it descended and stopped on Deck 6. Feeling extremely anxious, she turned to run to the stairs but heard another elevator ding. She rushed to it and waited, seemingly an eternity, before the door opened. It was empty. She rushed in and pushed Deck 6 button, then again and again. The door refused to shut. "God, god," she said and stomped her feet on the elevator floor. Finally, the door closed and the elevator descended to Deck 6. She hurried out and looked from side to side but did not see Mark. Several passengers milled around; some rushed to get the elevator up or down; some moved at a leisurely pace seemingly at peace and enjoying the amenities of the ship.

Determined to satisfy the anxiety that felt as if a knife was twisting back and forth at her insides, Kate decided to walk every inch of City Street and search every inch of every shop along the way. She hurried, moving from side to side to circumvent groups of people talking. Then she went into the pizza shop, looked from one side to the other and walked out. She looked in three or four shops, then crossed to the opposite side of the street.

She looked in the hot dog shop, then walked toward an open-front, dimly lit bar. Stopping suddenly, she gazed at the back of the bar that was illuminated by two LED signs and saw the back of a man with a multi-colored shirt with shorts. He walked into a room at the back of the bar. Just as quickly, a woman came to the front of the bar and turned off the bar lights, but the LED signs continued to be lit. The woman hurried to the back of the bar and disappeared into the room where the man had gone.

Kate felt her body go numb as if she had been shot in the back. She breathed deeply, then tiptoed into the bar being careful not to brush against a table or chair. The entrance to the room in the back of the bar was still illuminated by the signs, and she walked toward it, but it seemed to be miles away. Finally, though, she was at the doorway, and she leaned sideways into the opening with her right ear projected as far as possible. Noises came from a female, then from a male. Kate recognized the voice immediately. She had heard it in the café back home, on canoeing trips, on hiking trips, and in the suite on the boat. There was no mistaking that it was Mark. The noises became louder, and Kate froze as if in a trance. She wanted to scream. It was distinctly clear that Mark was having a sexual encounter with the woman.

Kate slowly backed away from the doorway, unconsciously feeling the tables and chairs to guide her exit from the bar. When she reached the street walkway, she walked fast, staring straight ahead but seeing nothing. She bumped into other passengers without knowing; she skirted groups of passengers without thinking; she hurried without a purpose. When her senses returned, she realized she was on the outer deck of the ship. Couples, hand in hand, walked past her, looked at her, but continued their walk. Other passengers looked over the side of the ship looking at the water in the darkness, and some pointed at a tiny light, miles away, of another ship.

Finding a section without passengers present, she walked to the rail and looked out into the darkness. Wanting to scream and cry at the same time, she refused to allow herself to do either one. She balanced herself with her arms on the rail and stared at the wake pattern as the ship sliced through the water. She watched without seeing the water rush away; noises were made by passengers talking, but she didn't hear them; the rush of the night air was chilly, but she didn't feel it.

Fifteen minutes passed. Suddenly, she stepped back and eased her grip on the rail. It was if a switch inside her head had been activated, and she could think again. The cool air swished by and brought a weird sound, a voice, strong and garbled but still a voice. *Avoid him and finish the cruise,* something or someone told her. She looked from side to side then behind her. In her confusion, she said, "Mom?"

CHAPTER 4

The cruise ship had docked in Miami at eight in the morning of the seventeenth. Because of all the requirements of disembarkation and flying to Nashville, she didn't get home until eleven at night. From the airport parking area, Mark had driven Kate to her car and waited until she was pulling off before he drove away. He had kissed her quickly on the cheek and said he would see her next week. She was glad he hadn't attempted to begin a big love fest to celebrate their being home because that would have required her to reject him. She didn't want to get into that kind of scenario so late at night.

When she got home, she immediately wrote in her journal.

September 17, 2002

Just returned from my cruise with Mark to the Caribbean. It was nice. Mark didn't feel well, so we didn't romance, which I will have to think about in the future. It's late, and I'm going to bed. Tomorrow's Wednesday, and I have to work. Will write more later. Signing off.

Five-thirty came early for Kate, but she bounded out of bed just as she always did when she was going to the café.

Kate got ready for work, then drove to the café. As she emerged from the car, she noticed that the morning was cooler than usual. *Fall is just around the corner,* she thought, *but there's still time for a hike in the mountains.* She opened the café door. As soon as she cleared the doorway, a loud chorus began: "Welcome home, Kate. We missed you." Bobbie, Sharon, and even Gill stood with open arms to hug her and welcome her back.

"Honey, how was your cruise?" Bobbie asked, her voice loud and reverberating around the room.

"It was wonderful! We just had the best big ol' time," Kate said.

"Your face has a glow about it," Bobbie said.

Kate laughed. "Well, I wouldn't go that far, but we did have a good time."

"We're all happy for you, honey."

"Yes, we are," Sharon said.

"Me too," Gill said.

Bobbie told Kate about everything that had happened since she left and what it was like working with Kate's mother again. Kate listened patiently, then they went to work getting ready for the day's business.

The day passed like the blink of the eye, or so it seemed to Kate. The remainder of the week passed just as quickly. Saturday night came and went, and she locked the door for her Sunday off. She got in her car and drove to the airport, parked in the Economy lot, took the shuttle to the rental car area, and walked to the counter of one of the most popular rental companies. She believed if something adverse happened with her future plans, she would not be remembered because of the volume of customers the rental company experienced.

"May I help you?" the rental agent said.

"Yes, I want to rent a standard car and return it Sunday night."

"Will this be business or personal rental?" the agent asked.

"Personal. My mechanic's working on my car Sunday, and I have a ton of things to do."

The agent looked at his monitor. "We have exactly what you want."

"Great! What color is it?"

"Color? That would be brown, but I can get you a black or a red."

"No, no, brown's perfect. Brown is my favorite color," Kate said, thinking that brown is sort of a neutral color and therefore not memorable.

"That's good. Just read the questions on the monitor in front of you, and you'll be on your way."

Kate completed the electronic contract, took the keys and found the assigned car, and drove home. It was completely dark now, and Kate believed that no one saw her in a different car. She went inside, got ready for bed, and then retired for the night.

The next morning, she pulled on a pair of jeans, made a cup of coffee for the road, and left home at five thirty. She drove onto I-40 and proceeded east. Kate was preoccupied, so the trip passed quickly, although it was nearly a three-hour drive. She took the exit to Cove Lake State Park, parked, and looked at the sharp, peaked mountaintop that was a backdrop for the peaceful water in the lake. *This is the most beautiful place on earth,* she thought.

She made a U-turn, drove back to I-75 and drove three miles to the top of the mountain. Seeing a scenic overlook, she pulled off and parked, then walked a trail that led to one of the mountain peaks. It was a quiet walk. Only a cawing hawk interrupted the tranquility. Brown and yellow leaves, having grown from tiny buds and taken their place as tiny specks in Mother Nature's scheme of life and death, now lay on the forest floor and soon would be only bits of matter. Some leaves dislodged themselves from the mother tree and drifted to the ground, twirling slowly as they fell and reflecting sun rays. On a casual day with the heart and head in peaceful moods, it would have been a period of introspection, indeed.

Passing a briar patch, she suddenly stopped, backed up, and stood for a full three minutes looking at the briars. She smiled and then continued her walk.

When she reached the mountaintop, she couldn't help but tell herself how the sprawling landscape created an uncommon sense of openness, gave an unobstructed view of the sky, and boasted a colorful carpet of trees and brush to top off its grandeur.

She walked off the trail to the edge of the mountaintop and looked down into a canyon that was littered with huge boulders and smaller rocks. A small sign was tacked to a tree that read: Eagle Point. The area where she stood was free of trees and brush and was a perfectly natural staging area for a photo shoot. She walked along the edge until she found an outcropping of rocks that was topped with a layer of flat rocks that were twelve to eighteen inches wide. *Perfect*, she thought.

She returned to the trail and found a stick that was an inch in diameter and three feet long, which she broke into three sections, and carried back to the spot with the thin layer of rocks. She bent over, then lay on her belly, and carefully began digging dirt and debris from the underside and around the first thin rock. Then she wiggled it until it was loose. She placed one stick below the loose rock and carefully placed the other end into the embankment below it, creating a temporary chock to hold the rock in place. Then she did the same with the rock next to it, and then the same for the adjoining third rock.

Carefully standing upright, she walked to a grove of trees and found four small limbs with leaves still attached, then returned to the open area and swept away all evidence of her lying on the ground. When she finished, she backed up to the trail sweeping her footprints away as she walked. She stood for a moment admiring her handiwork, then walked to a clump of trees and threw the limbs she had used into the underbrush. She returned to the trail and looked in all directions, making a mental note of the precise location that she had chosen; then she walked down the trail for five minutes and returned making a mental note of every root that crossed the trail, every limb or tree that encroached on the trail, and every rock that littered the trail.

After she had repeatedly reminded herself of the exact location of the area, she walked down the mountain to the rental car, then drove back to the airport to return it.

"How was the car, ma'am?" the rental agent asked.

"You know, it performed perfectly. In fact, I had a most prosperous day."

"I'm glad it turned out good for you."

"So am I."

Kate signed for the charge to her credit card, then took the shuttle to her car, drove home, and went inside. She dialed Mark.

"Hey, Kate! What a surprise!"

"And what a nice surprise to get you on the first ring. Do you have a minute?"

"For you, I have the whole day."

"One of my customers told me about a hiking trail in East Tennessee, and I know about it, but I had forgotten about it. It's beautiful! Has a lake with a beautiful peaked mountain behind it. Want to go for a hike Sunday?"

"That would be wonderful. I'll be back in town Thursday. Have to work Friday and see some clients on Saturday so Sunday will be a nice getaway."

"Great! Shall I fix breakfast at the café and then we'll head out?"

"Sounds like a plan. I'll see you on Sunday morning."

"Seven it is. See you then."

Kate worked through the week getting up every morning at five, getting ready for work, and reporting at six sharp for the day's activities. She told Bobbie that she and Mark were going hiking Sunday, and Bobbie told Sharon and Gill. Everyone was happy that she had found a soul mate.

After the lunch hour on Saturday, Kate went to the camera store, bought film and new batteries. She asked the store manager to test the camera. He teased her, assuming she was attending a really important event. She told him, no, just a hiking date. She also went to the deli department of the local grocery store and had them make deli sandwiches for the trip. The grocery clerk, Beatrice, told her that she was going to spoil Mark. Kate replied that she was trying her best to do just that.

Sunday came and Kate dressed in jeans and a long-sleeve cotton blouse; then she left the house and drove to the café, arriving at six-thirty. She prepared bacon, a bowl of fruit, orange juice, and coffee. At three minutes before seven, she scrambled eggs and made toast. Mark as usual appeared at seven on the dot.

"Everything's still hot," he said.

"All because of my great planning," she said.

They laughed.

Kate prepared two plates, and they had a leisurely breakfast. At ten minutes before eight, they left the café and drove over the Cumberland Mountains to East Tennessee. Kate told Mark that she believed the lake and mountaintop was the Cove Lake exit, so they took the exit and sure enough, the mountain peak rose majestically behind the lake.

"It's like a painting," Mark said. "I've never seen anything quite so beautiful. It's like you might see in Colorado or at Lake Tahoe."

"Stop, and I'll make a picture so we can remember the hike up that mountain," Kate said. "If it turns out good, I'll have it enlarged and framed so you can put it in your most favorite place at home."

Mark looked at her, and his eyebrows raised. "I'd like that very much," he said, and then guided the car onto the shoulder of the highway and parked.

"This is perfect," Kate said as she opened the passenger-side door. She got out, walked to a spot between the highway and Mark's car, positioned herself, and took three shots of the mountain, and then she returned to the car and got in. "Wanna see?" she asked, then turned the camera screen for Mark to see.

"Absolutely. Oh, my gosh! It's beautiful! It's gorgeous! What a beautiful picture that will be hanging on my wall!"

"I'm glad you like it. Okay, ready to hike?"

"Ready. Where to?"

"My customer said to take I-75 about three miles from this exit, and there's a scenic view parking area on the right side."

"We're off," Mark said then drove back to the interstate and three miles north.

"Stop! Stop! I bet that's it," Kate said, motioning to the same area that she had visited a week before.

Mark turned in to the parking area and parked. "These are beautiful mountains," he said.

"I love 'em," Kate said.

They got out of the car, did some stretching exercises, and started the hike up the trail to the mountaintop.

"Wait, wait! I forgot my camera!" Kate said, her voice sounding almost in panic mode.

"I'll get it," Mark said.

"No! No! I'll get it! May I have the keys to the car?"

"Here you are."

Kate took the keys and ran back to the car. She got the camera, made sure it was loaded; she then returned to the spot where Mark waited and returned the keys to him. "I didn't want to miss some good shots when we get to the top," she said, breathless.

They resumed their walk along the trail. "I'm really pleased and happy that you invited me to see this beautiful place, Kate."

"Wait until we get to the top. I was told it's the most beautiful vista this side of the Mississippi."

"Can't wait. This is quite an arduous climb, isn't it?"

"It's almost straight up," Kate said, "but we're true mountain people, so we'll make it."

Mark laughed. "Right."

They walked for another thirty minutes and then reached the top.

"One hour and twenty-five minutes from bottom to top," Mark said. "Whoa! This is the place! We're on top of the world!"

Kate smiled. "This is gorgeous! I'm so glad my customer reminded me about this place," Kate said.

They ambled along the trail long enough to catch their breath; then Mark said, "I have to look over the side of the mountain. Want to come?"

Kate hesitated for a moment, then said, "I wouldn't miss it."

They walked to the edge of the mountaintop, and Mark held onto a tree branch and peeked down into the canyon. "This is remarkable," he said. "Want to take a peek?"

"Sure. Is that limb pretty strong?"

"It held me, but I'll hold your hand if you want to look."

It suddenly struck Kate that Mark may have conceived a plan of his own to do her harm on the mountaintop, so she said, "I'll hold the limb."

Mark laughed and said, "Okay."

Kate held the limb and looked over the edge of the mountaintop into the canyon. "What a magnificent view!" she said, her voice loud and echoing off the canyon walls. She stepped back and steadied herself before letting go of the limb. "Shall we continue?" she said.

"Let's. I'm primed to walk."

They continued walking until they reached the location that Kate had visited the prior week. The area near the edge of the mountaintop was clear of trees and brush. Standing on the trail, it appeared that this part of the mountain came to an abrupt halt in its evolution, and a second, taller section of the mountain evolved creating a gigantic backdrop to the first section. In between the two sections, of course, was an endless canyon layered with rocks. It was as if hundreds of dump trucks had rolled to the edge of the first mountaintop and dumped huge, jagged boulders that covered the walls and bottom of the canyon.

"Mark! Mark! Look! Look at the beautiful scene! See how that mountaintop rises from this one."

"Wow! Now, that's a picture!"

"Come on. I have to make a picture of you standing with that mountaintop behind you," Kate said, then she ran off the trail to the cleared area. She looked hurriedly to locate the three rocks that she had loosened from the dirt, and her heart beat faster when she saw them lying innocently on the ground forming an apparent strong edge of the cliff. "Here! Here's a perfect place!" she yelled and motioned for him to come to her.

Mark jogged to the open area and said, "Beautiful! Where do I stand?"

"Let me get the best view…there…perfect. Okay, stand straight in front of me."

Mark moved over so that he appeared to be straight in front of Kate's camera lens.

"A little to your left," Kate said.

Mark moved slightly to his left.

"A little more…about a foot."

He moved his left foot to his left then moved his right foot the same distance.

"Perfect! Now, back up just a little."

Mark looked behind him. "I don't want to fall in that deep hole," he said.

Kate giggled. "You're not going to fall, silly. There's a layer of rocks just behind you."

"Okay, I'm backing up," he said, then put his left foot on one of the rocks. "All right," he said, the wrinkles in his brow smoothing out as he became confident of the safety in his footing. He placed his other foot on a second rock and instantly began to teeter slowly back and forth. He flung his hands into the air searching for support, but his arms and hands just flailed in the air.

Kate took a step toward him but stayed out of this reach.

Suddenly, the rocks broke loose from the embankment. Mark seemed to be attached to the rocks for a moment, but his body instantly tilted backward. It was as if he were standing upright with his back to a bed and then fallen backward onto the bed. As rapidly as a flashing picture, he was prone in the air, then disappeared.

Kate moved closer to the edge of the cliff and peered over just in time to see his body slam into the side of the jagged cliff, ricochet off, fall farther, then slam again into the cliff. It seemed an interminable amount of time before he finally crashed to the bottom of the canyon. He came to rest face up on a huge boulder.

Kate backed up and yelled, "Help! Help!" She ran to the trail and started down the mountain screaming, "Help! Help!" Seeing the briar patch just ahead, she put her hands over her eyes and ran straight into the patch for a distance of six feet and exited the other end. Hundreds of bacteria-laden barbs ripped the flesh on her arms, midsection, and legs, causing blood to run freely. Some of the barbs pricked the tips of her ears, and blood ran down the side of her face. The pain was intense, and she screamed at the top of her voice as she continued to run. Even with the extreme pain, she suddenly thought about her blood loss. With all her planning, she hadn't considered the consequences of injuring herself, and she immediately became scared.

She ran faster ignoring the downward slope and her footing. Her ankles turned from right to left as her feet struck uneven surfaces. Sharp pains shot up her ankles and legs. She turned her head and saw her bloody arm, and then panicked. She screamed as loudly as she could, but her voice was now weak and strained from the constant screaming. Her sounds were barely audible.

She tripped and lunged toward a tree but stuck out her hands and caught herself before crashing head-first into the tree. The near tragic fall rattled her thoughts, but she was weak and the realization that she could have been killed did not fully register in her brain. The pain in her arms was excruciating. Blood caked on her arms and acted like glue holding her blouse and skin together. She staggered back onto the trail.

"Miss...Miss, are you okay?" asked a young man who was wearing a backpack and carrying a walking stick.

"Shawn, she's not okay," a second man said, his words sounding hurried. "Throw her arm around your neck. I'll get the other arm. Act like we're carrying her off the football field. Let's go! Get this lady off the mountain!"

Holding Kate between them, the men began to run, dragging her feet along the dirt trail. Her head dropped to one side and rested precariously on her shoulder.

"She's out! Run! Run! I'm calling nine-one-one," the second man yelled; he then wrestled with his cell phone. "Slow down for a second," he yelled, and then dialed the number.

"Nine-one-one," a female voice said.

"Emergency! Emergency! We have a lady covered with blood! She needs an ambulance! She's passed out! Hurry! Hurry!"

"We have your location. An ambulance will arrive in fifteen minutes," the woman said.

"An ambulance is coming in fifteen minutes! Let's go! Don't die on us, lady. Please don't die."

It took eighteen minutes for the two men to reach the bottom of the mountain. Kate's body was limp. They laid her down gently in a grassy area.

An ambulance blared in the distance as the men hurried through the green and brown weeds that formed the fringe area of the mountain. Sticky weed seeds stuck to the hair on their legs, and other strong-stemmed weeds scratched their legs and ankles before they reached the gravel area along the edge of the highway.

The ambulance drove alongside and pulled to a stop in front of them. Two men jumped out, opened the rear doors of the ambulance, and pulled out a wheeled stretcher.

"Did she fall?" one of the ambulance techs asked.

"We don't know. We just found her halfway up the mountain," one of the hikers said.

"Yeah, she was in really bad shape," the second hiker said.

"Do you know if anyone else was with her?" the ambulance tech asked.

"We don't know."

"Follow us to the hospital. You may have to fill out a police report," the ambulance tech said.

CHAPTER 5

"She'll come around soon," the hospital nurse said to the two sheriff deputies. "She doesn't have any broken bones. Her vitals are okay, but she was dehydrated when we got her. The IV's taking care of that. We cleaned her up and gave her a tetanus shot and some antibiotics. She has some bad lacerations. Looks like she got caught in a bramble patch. We treated all the scratches, some of them really deep. She's really lucky. If those two young men hadn't found her, she might not have made it off the mountain. She needs a coupla days' rest."

"We'll wait until she wakes up," one of the deputies said. "We need to find out if something happened in the mountains. Sorta weird for a woman to be in the mountains passed out and bloody, wouldn't you say?"

"I would," the hospital tech said.

"Could be a tragedy happened up there or something onerous," one of the deputies said, then stretched out his legs and closed his eyes.

The second deputy looked at him, then did the same.

Fifty minutes passed. Suddenly, Kate's eyes opened slightly, and she made a gurgling sound.

One of the deputies, roused from his nap, looked at her. "She's waking up. Better get the nurse," he said and elbowed the second deputy.

The second deputy jerked, then jumped up and hurried out of the room. He returned with a nurse.

"Hey, welcome back. We were worried about you," the nurse said.

"Wher...where am I?" Kate said, her voice barely audible.

"You're in a hospital. I'm taking care of you. You were pretty scratched up from head to toe. What happened to you?"

"Mark..." Kate said, almost in a whisper.

"Can you say that again, honey?" the nurse said.

"Mark," Kate said.

"Mark?" the hospital tech said.

"He fell...off...the mountain," Kate said, her words slow and muffled.

"Mark fell off the mountain?" the tech said.

"Yes."

"Who's Mark?" the tech asked.

"My...fi...fiancé."

"Where? Where did Mark fall off the mountain?"

"Eag...Eagle Po..."

"Eagle Point?"

"Yes."

"Is he still there?"

"Yes."

One of the deputies pulled a telephone from his utility belt and walked out of the room into the hallway. His voice was loud and could be heard several feet away. "Yes, we're going up to Eagle Point. There may be an injured citizen up there. We're going to take the two men that found the woman. They'll be able to show us where the woman came from."

The deputy listened for a moment then said, "Ten-four, over and out."

CHAPTER 6

Kate stayed in bed at the hospital for two days. She answered dozens of questions posed by the Sheriff's Department. "We were just taking a hike," she told them. "I was preparing to take a picture of Mark, and he just backed up too far and fell off. I was horrified. It was like I just immediately went into shock and started running. I didn't know where I was going. I just ran. I screamed and screamed for help," she had said and started crying to add credence to her grief. The deputies told her that it was just a tragic accident and that they would write it up as such.

She had talked to her mother the night after she awakened and told her of the catastrophe on the mountain but refused to let her mother come to the hospital to see her. "Mother, I'll see you at home. No, you're not coming here," she had told her.

She also called Bobbie and told her the deputies had found Mark, and he was deceased. Bobbie was overcome with grief and asked if it was possible for her and Sharon to attend the funeral. "Of course you'll come. We'll close the day of the funeral. How can we stay open?

He was the love of my life."

On Day 3, following the tragedy, Kate was released from the hospital. Mark's car had been impounded by the Sheriff's Department, so she had a taxi take her to a car rental lot where she rented a car. Then she drove to Nashville International Airport, returned the rental car, and called her mom. "Mom, I'm at the airport. Will you pick me up and take me home?"

"I will, but I warn you…I'm not in a good mood. The way you treated me while you were in the hospital was the worst thing that's ever happened to me."

"Mom, I'll explain when you pick me up."

"You will?"

"I will. Now, hurry. I've been in the hospital for nearly three days, and I've had it."

"You were there for two days."

"Okay, two days in bed and a third day wasting time. I was there for three days. Now, please come and get me."

"I'll be there in fifteen minutes. Where will you be?"

"Departure deck. All the way down at Southwest check-in."

"Okay. Goodbye."

"Bye," Kate said. She then took the escalator to the departure deck floor, walked outside, and waited at the curb.

Eighteen minutes passed before her mother drove up to the curb. Kate got in. "Hello, mother."

"So, Mark didn't treat you right?"

"Mother…"

"I'm your mother, and I know all. I raised you to fend for yourself; I raised you to take action if a man abused you; I raised you to be strong. You're my daughter. By the way, your fiancé's family is receiving friends and family at Beech and West Funeral Home tonight beginning at seven. Funeral's at eleven tomorrow in the chapel. I suppose you want me to stay away from both events?"

"Of course not. You're my mother. I want you at my side. I'll pick you up at six, and we'll meet Mark's parents."

"Yes, dear."

"Any problems at the café?"

"Everything's perfect at the café. I have a lot of experience, you know."

"I know. Please wear your black dress with the high, round neck."

"Of course, dear." Sara smiled as she guided her car to Kate's home.

Once the car came to a stop, Kate got out and told her mother she would see her at six. She then hurried up to the steps and used the entry fob to open the door. The foyer was spacious, measuring ten feet by ten feet. A huge mahogany table sat in the center of the space. It held a porcelain eagle in flight mounted on dark, three-inch, mounded material that was the size of a dinner plate. Kate had bought it right away as she associated it with her flight to freedom.

She walked to her desk, pulled out her journal and began writing.

October 4, 2002

Dear Journal,

I've missed you because I've been gone for several days. During that time, I was swept away by a tide of emotions. I thought on several occasions that I might drown in the sea of despair, but I pulled myself up and flew like a colorful bird to a mountaintop where I tripped along in a soothing mist of tranquility. Mark, in his world of inadequacy, attempted to glide alongside me, but the Invisible Hand in all his wisdom swooped down and took Mark away as if he were a person in the darkness of deceit and possessed with mental corruptness. Tonight my mother and I will view his body, and I will bid him adieu as he begins his journey through infinite travels of murky space.

I will sign off on this most auspicious occasion.

Kate carefully placed the journal in the desk drawer then went out to the kitchen, and made a sandwich and a cup of coffee for herself. She sat down by the window that overlooked the backyard. She took a bite of the sandwich and looked out at the trees. The weather was drifting into autumn; red and yellow leaves separated from their mother trees and twirled slowly to the ground. As the sun peeked through the tops of the trees, it cast bright rays at irregular intervals on the ground.

Kate finished eating, put her dishes away, took a shower, and then applied a conservative amount of makeup on her cheeks. She looked through her closet, chose a black dress with a high neckline and black pumps. She looked through her jewelry and selected a pearl necklace. She dressed at a leisurely pace, then looked at herself in a full-length mirror. "You look like you're going to a funeral," she said, then she locked up and drove to her mother's home. Before she could even stop the car, her mother appeared on her front porch, walked down to Kate's car, and got in.

"Hi, Mother, you look pretty."

"And so do you. In fact, we look alike."

"Like mother, like child."

Sara smiled.

Kate drove to the funeral home, then she and her mother got out and walked toward the entrance. "Mother, when we meet Mark's parents, I'm going to be emotional…perhaps cry. When I do, I want you to put your arms around me and console me."

"Like a good mother would?"

"Yes, like a good mother."

"Then I will certainly act like a good mother, and I will start by opening the door for you."

As Sara reached for the door, it suddenly opened.

"Please come in," a man with graying hair said.

Kate looked at him, but the dim light from the interior of the room caused the man to appear as a spooky character in a horror movie. Dressed in a black suit and black tie, he was six feet tall with a bulging stomach. He spoke in a muffled tone.

"I'm Walter Beech, the funeral director. Are you here for the visitation of Mark Simmons?"

"Uh, Mark, we're here for Mark," Kate said.

"What a charming fellow he was and what a terrible accident. What relation are you?"

"I was…or, uh, I was his fiancée."

"Please accept my condolences. Mr. and Mrs. Simmons are in the Magnolia Room. May I take you to them?"

"Please. Mother…"

"I'm so sorry. Your mother?"

"Yes."

Walter extended both arms and took Sara's hand in his. "I am so sorry. Please forgive my rudeness."

"Walter, it's okay," Sara said.

"My apologies again. Please follow me."

Kate and Sara followed Walter to a couple standing beside a table that had a large framed photograph of Mark situated squarely in its center.

"Mr. and Mrs. Simmons?"

A dark-haired woman, slightly shorter than Kate, turned. "Yes?"

"I'm Kate."

"Kate! Oh, Kate!" she said and extended her arms.

Kate took a step forward and felt Mrs. Simmons' arms go around her neck. She extended her own arms and touched the woman's shoulders.

"I'm so sorry," Kate whispered, then thought of herself as sad, and tears flowed slowly down her cheeks.

"Mark talked so much about you. He told me every time the two of you did something together."

"I'll miss him so much."

"Please forgive me. This is Matt, Mark's father, and I'm Martha."

Matt extended his arms and held Kate. "Can we do anything…anything at all for you?" he said.

"I just have to work through this tragedy," Kate said.

"Do you want to see Mark?" Matt asked. "They had to do so much to his face. The impact of the fall crushed his skull."

Kate held Matt's hand, then turned to her mother. "Please come with us, Mother."

Sara joined them, and they walked to the casket. Kate looked down at Mark and thought of the cruise and what a deceitful creature he had been. "We'll miss you," she said as tears filled the corners of her eyes. She felt an arm go around her waist, so she turned and realized that it was her mother. "It's going to be so empty without him," Kate said and looked into her mother's eyes.

"I know you will, darling. We'll be here to help you though. Do you want to meet the other people who have come to share their condolences?"

"Yes, Mother, I do," Kate said taking her mother's hand.

They talked with every person who came to the funeral home to offer their condolences and pay their respects; then they visited Matt and Martha, expressed once again their pain and sorrow, excused themselves, and left the funeral home.

They got into Kate's car, and Kate began driving toward Sara's home.

"You were respectful, honey, and quite convincing."

"Mother!"

"Just an observation."

Kate drove the remaining mile to her mother's home, her mother got out, and wished her a good night.

"You'll be ready to go tomorrow?" Kate said.

"Of course, honey."

Kate drove to her home, went inside, had coffee and a dry piece of toast, and went to bed.

The next day, she drove to her mother's home, and Sara was waiting in the driveway. She walked hastily to the car and got in. "Good morning, my angel."

"Good morning, Mother. You're going to catch a cold standing out in this chilly air," Kate said.

"I didn't want you to wait on me."

"You've always been a great mother. You've always looked out after me."

Sara smiled. "Did you sleep well?"

"Like a log. You?"

"Like an old log," Sara said.

"Mother! You're still a young chicken."

"Ha."

They drove to the funeral home, attended the service for Mark, then joined the procession to the cemetery and attended a short service there.

After the service, her mother whispered that she wanted to visit another gravesite, and she would return shortly; then she walked down a small slope, around a tree, and disappeared.

Kate watched as the attendees walked to their cars; then she spotted a four-leaf clover and bent down and picked it. Still kneeling and admiring the plant, she felt something touch her shoulder. Believing it to be her mother, she started to stand, but a man's voice said, "Kate."

She stood erect, turned to look at the man, and said, "Mr. Mayor."

"I'm sorry for your loss," he said, then embraced her.

Kate felt uncomfortable. "Thank you."

"Will it be okay if I drop in the café from time to time and have coffee…maybe talk with you?"

What an odd request, Kate thought, but she said, "Sure, Mr. Mayor. We'd like to have you."

He smiled broadly. "Good! Good! I'll see you soon, and again, I'm sorry for your loss."

CHAPTER 7

Kate stayed home and away from the café on Friday and Saturday following the funeral to give herself a break and avoid the crowd of she anticipated would visit the café to pay their respects. Feeling that time would erase some memories, she called Bobbie and told her she was taking off the following week to recuperate. The week passed, and the tragic death of Mark had become a leaf in the history of the community.

On Monday morning, she drove to the café arriving at six o'clock. She walked in and reminded herself that it had been a full week since she had worked.

"Honey, are you okay?" Bobbie asked, her forehead and cheeks showing wrinkles from her concern.

The voice startled Kate, and she turned awkwardly. "Bobbie, I...I didn't know you were here," she said.

"How're you doing, honey?"

"I'm fine. It's going to take a little time to get back in the groove."

"Of course it will. Is there anything we can do to help you?"

"No, no, I'm fine."

"The mayor came in asking about you on Friday."

"The mayor?"

"Yeah, and he acted real concerned that you weren't here."

"He spoke to me at the cemetery, and said he'd stop in from time to time to check on us."

"Now, that's really nice of the mayor."

"Yes, it is, and I'm dying for a cup of coffee."

"It's made, honey. I'll get you a cup."

Kate had coffee, a biscuit with jelly, then reacquainted herself with the chores and responsibilities of the café.

"Kate."

Without turning to look, Kate knew the voice was the mayor's. She remembered from the cemetery that the voice was precise, almost sharp. He was a perfect representation of an Italian man—dark curly hair, tan complexion, and a long, sharp nose. His bubbly, extroverted personality contributed to his charm, which won him the mayorship by eliminating the competition before the race had begun.

Kate turned to him and said, "Yes, sir."

"How are you? I started worrying about you, so I came right over."

"I'm fine. Everyone has been very gracious."

"I'm glad. I wouldn't want to pass a proclamation on your behalf."

Kate smiled.

"Kate, I have something to talk with you about. Do you mind if we step outside? It's sort of a private matter."

Kate's eyes squinted as if she were puzzled. "Sure." She walked out of the café to the corner of the building away from the sight of the windows.

"Mr. Mayor, here we are. Why did you want to talk to me?"

The mayor reached out and held Kate's right arm with both his hands. "Please call me Mike. It's a long way from Mario, but Mike's what my best friends call me. Kate, I know you're going through rough times, and I want to help you. I have a cabin on the lake. It's really secluded. Would you like to go out there and just kick back and relax…like the end of the week?"

Kate looked at him and frowned. "Mr. Mayor, uh Mike, your wife would have me strung up at noon if I did that."

"Oh, no, no! She's restricted to quarters. Has lupus. She'll probably never go to the cabin again."

"Your wife has lupus?"

"Yes, but I have someone taking care of her. She'll never want for anything."

"Mr. Mayor, uh Mike, this is a very unusual situation. I'm afraid I'll have to have some time to think about your invitation, and you'll have to agree that it certainly is not fair to your wife."

"Oh, please," he said, holding her arm tighter.

Kate stepped backward and said, "You have very strong hands."

His eyes enlarged, and he said, "I'm so sorry! Did I hurt you? It would be terrible if I did."

"No, no, I'm okay."

"Good! I'll drop back by the end of the week. That'll give you some time to think about everything."

"Okay. Have a good day," Kate said, then walked back into the café as a hundred thoughts raced through her head.

"Honey, are you okay?" Bobbie asked. "We thought you'd run away."

"Yes, I'm okay. I was outside talking with the mayor."

"The mayor?"

"Yes, he wanted to make sure I was okay."

"Honey, I don't want to stick my nose in your business, but you have to be careful with the mayor."

"Careful. Why careful?"

"Well, you know—well, there's just no other way to say it. He's a womanizer, and that's just no good."

"A womanizer?"

"Yes, he has a long list of accomplishments here in town."

"Bobbie, thank you. I'll be careful. Hey, we have to get ready for the morning rush, don't we? See, I still remember what goes on here at the ol' café."

Bobbie laughed.

As the day progressed, Kate was shocked at the number of patrons visiting the café, and the number of visitors grew so much that it was difficult to get in and out of the building. Everyone offered their condolences and asked if Kate was alright. She assured them that she was okay, and even though there was an empty spot in her heart with the loss of Mark, she had to continue with her life.

The day blew by like a whirlwind, and each following day sped by just as rapidly. Kate felt as if she were on a roller coaster, and with the days blending together, Friday came in a flash. She reminded herself of the day and still did not know what she would do if the mayor showed up. It would be a miracle if he got involved in city business and forgot about her.

At precisely ten o'clock, however, he entered the café. "Good morning! Did you save a cup of coffee for the mayor?"

"Yes, we did. Coffee, one cream and no sugar. Coming up," Kate said.

He smiled then took a small notepad from his pocket and wrote something and showed it to Kate. It read, "Did you think about tonight?"

Kate read it, hesitated for a moment and said, "I did."

He smiled broadly and said, "And?"

"What time and where?"

He smiled again and then started writing on a clean sheet from his notepad. When he finished, he tore the sheet away from the pad and offered it to Kate.

She took it from him and looked at it. It read, "See you at 8:30 p.m. Take interstate west to River Road exit, then go north on River Road to the second road on right. The cabin is a one-quarter mile on right. Road dead-ends at the cabin."

Kate looked up, hesitated for a moment, and then said, "I'll see you there."

The mayor again smiled broadly and said, "Okay! Okay!" He gulped down his coffee and hurried out of the café.

Hmm, what will I wear to see the mayor who is cheating on his wife? I'll think about that somewhere around six.

The morning passed quickly, and the lunch hour came and went just as quickly. It was a typical Friday. Many of the customers had a quick lunch and headed home for the weekend. Most were happy because it was payday.

After all the customers had left, Kate and the crew had their lunch at the table that faced the door—the same table they had used since Kate took over ownership and the same table Kate's mother and her crew had used.

At home, Kate freshened up and changed into jeans and a blouse-shirt, the bottom ends of which she tied in a knot and caused the shirt to fall just below the top of her jeans. She looked at herself in a full-length mirror, turned sideways, and looked again. "Looks pretty good," she said. "Well, let's see what the mayor has on his mind."

She left home, drove to the interstate, and followed the directions until she arrived at the cabin. The mayor was standing on the shoulder of the driveway. When he saw the headlights of her car, he walked to the center of the driveway and held up his hands. She braked, and he stepped over to the driver's side of her car and motioned to her to lower her window.

She rolled down the window. "Something wrong?"

"No, no," he said in a soft tone, "but drive to the back of the cabin and park in the garage. One bay is open for you."

She squinted at him but drove to the back and slowly pulled into the stand-alone garage. "Can't let wifey know," she said softly.

The mayor rushed to the car and opened the door. "That's great," he said. "When we get out of the garage, I'll let the door down."

"Okay, I don't think anyone's going to steal it though."

"You can never be too careful," he said. "Come, come, let's go inside."

They exited the garage, and he used a remote to close the door. When they walked up to the cabin, he rushed to open the door.

"Let there be light," he said, then flipped the switch for the lights. Even with the lights on, it was very dark and difficult to see. The mayor had apparently invested in twenty-five-watt bulbs. "Do you want to sit at the bar or is it too high for you?"

"Bar's good."

"Kate, I'm so happy you decided to come. It means so much to me. I have a birthday soon. Wouldn't it be great to be able to celebrate here at this beautiful place?"

"A birthday. Why, Mayor, you'll be another year older."

He laughed. "May I get you a drink...maybe a glass of wine?"

"A glass of wine would be great. Do you have anything with a 2011 date? That was a great year for grapes in California."

"My wine makes California look cheap."

Kate laughed. "Just pulling your leg, Mr. Mayor...Mike. Anything you have will be great."

He filled a jumbo wine glass half-full and held it out for Kate. "I think you'll enjoy this."

"Thank you," Kate said, and then sipped the wine. "It is good." She leaned back and supported herself on the back of the chair.

The mayor poured himself a glass, looked at Kate, and said, "Do you know I've adored you from the day I first saw you. You were eighteen, just graduated from high school. If you remember, I gave the commencement address."

"I remember very well. When you shook my hand, you held it for a long time," Kate said.

"I did. I was mesmerized by you...just your presence. Your very presence in the room caused it to light up. I mean there was magic when you walked into a room. Here, let me give you a refill." He took Kate's glass and filled it to the halfway mark and gave it back to her. "Let's sit on the couch. It's much more comfortable than these ridiculously high bar stools."

The ol' couch routine, Kate thought. *Only took you about five minutes to get around to it.*

She walked to the couch and sat down, perching her wine glass on her knee.

The mayor hurried over and sat down close to Kate. "Don't you like the quietness and privacy of this place? It's like you just left all civilization behind."

"And it's quite dark."

"Purposely. I did that purposely. It adds to the aura of this little world, don't you think?"

"I agree it's quiet; it's private; it's dark."

When she lifted her wine glass for a sip, he put his hand just above her knee.

"Mr. Mayor! You're getting fresh."

"Oh, I didn't mean to offend you," he said quickly, "but I'm just spellbound by your beauty."

"Mr. Mayor, let's cut to the chase. Before we leave here, you want us to wind up in that bedroom of yours. I'm sorry to inform you that you picked the wrong week if you know what I mean."

The mayor's eyebrows raised, and his cheeks tightened as if he had been slapped.

"Mr. Mayor, I have to get going. I have to open the café tomorrow."

"Do you really have to go? I was hoping we could have another wine and talk."

"I do have to go. Saturday's the worst day of the week."

"Okay, let me walk you to your car. Is it okay if I drop in and see you next week?"

"Mr. Mayor, we have to be sensible. If you frequent my place so that it's noticeable to the regulars, people are going to talk; your position could be in jeopardy; your wife could be hurt."

"But I'd be just another customer—a regular."

"Well, visit at your own peril." She walked quickly through the cabin to the door as the mayor tried to keep up.

"I can't wait until Monday," he said.

"Monday it is!" Kate said, then walked to her car, got in, and drove home. After she'd locked up for the night, she headed straight to her desk. She pulled out her journal, took a deep breath, and began writing.

October 18, 2002

Dear Journal:

In the prior days of my life, I have managed to scale the highest peak of the highest mountain and cement my well-being into an impenetrable vault that guaranteed safety for my confidence and the genes that my mother so graciously shared with me.

Tonight, I betrayed the invincible will that has shaped and molded me into the person I am—the person I'm proud to know and the person that dwells in my heart that I cherish and hold and honor with the greatest honor and respect.

I regret this misstep with great sorrow.

CHAPTER 8

As Kate drove to the café Saturday morning, she thought about the night with the mayor. She regretted agreeing to go see him because it only gave the mayor the impression that she was available to him, that she was willing to have sex with him, and that he could drop into her life whenever he wanted. "Damn!" she said.

She arrived at fifteen minutes after six, a little later than normal. She parked in back and was walking to the entrance when Bobbie burst out of the café and ran toward her.

"Honey," Bobbie said, then paused long enough to get a breath, "the mayor came by..." She paused again and took a deep breath. "He's looking for you, wants you to come to City Hall soon as you get here."

Kate looked at her. "What in the world for?"

"I don't know, honey. He just wanted you to come."

"It's a quarter after six. I don't have time to run all over town to see the mayor. I have a café to run. Doesn't the mayor know that...or care?"

"I can manage without you if you want to go see him, honey," Bobbie said.

"Oh, okay, thank you." Kate walked back to her car, drove to City Hall, and parked. She got out, walked into the building and down the hallway that led to the mayor's office. Framed pictures of The Great Smokey Mountains, Tennessee walking horses, East Tennessee farmland, and country music stars seemed to breathe life into the walls along the way.

She peeked around the corner into the mayor's office and saw that he was occupied with another person.

Seeming to sense that Kate was there, the mayor looked up. When he saw her, he sprang to his feet and rushed to the door. "Kate! Kate!" he said and reached for her hand.

Taken aback by the sudden rush, Kate backed up and looked at him and studied the expression in his face and eyes. "Mr. Mayor, you have someone with you. I'll be back."

"No! No! Hold on," he said, then hurried in and said something to the man in a low voice.

The man's head turned quickly toward the door where Kate stood; he got up and walked brusquely out of the office.

The mayor motioned for Kate to come in, then closed the door as soon as Kate stepped across the threshold.

"I'm so happy to see you!" he said. "I couldn't sleep last night. I just tossed back and forth thinking about you. I want to see you every day this week and every day next week and every day thereafter. If you will honor me with your presence, I want to have another night with you at the cabin Friday night."

A thousand thoughts sped through Kate's head, but she finally said, "Mr. Mayor…Mr. Mayor, uh, there's no way to see you every day except at the café, and as I told you last night, that would not be a good idea. People would catch on really fast, and that would be the end of your career and your marriage."

"But, but, but, I have to see you. I mean, I think about you every second, every minute. I see you even though you're not here. A portrait of you is in my head. You're my angel."

"Just come for lunch on Friday and pretend that's the only reason you're there."

"What about calling you?"

"My phone has texting capability. Text me."

"And I just got a phone with texting capability. Text you I will!"

"But only once a day. I'm really busy at the café."

"Okay, once daily. I'll read your text over and over until the next day."

"I have to get back to work."

The mayor reached out to hold her.

"Mr. Mayor, we're at the City Hall. You can't do that here…later," Kate said, then walked out the office, down the hallway, out of the building, and got into her car. She sat for a moment processing every minute of what she had just experienced; then she started the car, put it in gear, and started driving. She looked straight ahead as she drove by buildings, streets, and then into the suburbs. The car seemed to pilot itself as it zoomed by house after house, and then it pulled into a driveway. Kate got out of the car, walked up the steps to the house, and knocked on the door.

After a few seconds, the door opened. "Kate?"

"Yes, it's Kate. May I come in?"

"Of course you can come in. My only daughter is welcome anytime. Now, your mother is very perceptive though. For one, you're at your mother's house early in the morning when your first love is the café. So, out with it. What's going on?"

"Mom, I have a big problem."

"Big problems are men. Who is it?"

"The mayor."

"The mayor?" Sara said, her voice sounding as if she were choking. "Like the mayor of our city or the mayor of another city?" She struggled to get the words out.

"This city."

After inhaling and gaining her composure, Sara said, "And what seems to be the problem."

"I made the mistake of visiting him at his cabin Friday night. No, I didn't go to bed with him, and I don't want to and never will. I just came from City Hall. He wants to see me every day; he can't stop thinking about me; he wants me to come to the cabin Friday night. He's going to cause me a lot of problems, Mom; he's going to suffocate me; he wants to possess me."

Sara put her arms around Kate and pulled her close. "When do you see him again, honey?"

"He's coming for lunch at the café on Friday."

"Friday? Around noontime?"

"Yes."

"Honey, leave it to your mother. You get back to the café. Keep your chin up and point your nose into the wind. Your dilemma's practically solved."

"It is?"

"Practically solved. Oh, by the way, I want you to make a big batch of banana pudding for Friday. Now, get out. Go! Go!" Sara said, smiling.

"Banana pudding, huh. Alright. Thank you. I'm gone." Kate hugged her mother, left her house, and started driving to the café. Suddenly, she yelled, "Oh, my god!" She checked her phone, which had no messages, then made a U-turn and sped back to her mother's house. Before the car had come to a complete stop, she forced the gear into park, jumped out, ran up the steps, and beat on her mother's door. The door jerked open. "What is it? What is it?" her mother asked, turning an ashen color.

"Mom…Mom, whatever you're doing, can you do it tomorrow?" Kate said, her words high-pitched. She sounded near hysteria.

Her mother hesitated for a moment as the color in her face began returning. "I'll have to get busy, but, yes, honey…Tuesday, Tuesday it is. Concentrate and listen to me. You must today tell the mayor you're having banana pudding on Tuesday, and you must make a big deal of it when you serve it on Tuesday, and tell him not to come for lunch until one o'clock."

"Oh, Mother, thank you, thank you! I've got to run. Lunch on Tuesday. Banana pudding served. Don't come to lunch until one o'clock. Got it!"

She hurried out and drove as fast as she could to City Hall. She parked very near the steps that led to the courthouse, jumped out of the car, and charged into the building and down the hallway to the mayor's office. As she was about to turn the corner and enter the office, the mayor appeared in front of her. She held out her hand, touched his chest, and pushed him backward into his office.

"Kate?"

"Into your office, Mr. Mayor."

"What a pleasant surprise!" he said. "I was just about to text you."

"Don't! Whatever you do, don't text me and don't call me."

"I thought..."

"Change of plans. Instead of texting me, instead of calling me, instead of electronically communicating with me in any shape, form, or fashion, don't! Instead of all those things, come to lunch today, come to lunch tomorrow, come to lunch the next day and the next day and the next day. Don't text, don't call, come to lunch. Any questions?"

"No, you've covered it all, much to my satisfaction. I'll be there between twelve and twelve-thirty."

"Make it one o'clock. Make it one o'clock every day. Today and every day, make it one. Is that okay with you?"

"Yes, it's great with me. One o'clock every day. That'll work better for me anyway. My secretary can go from twelve to one, and I'll go at one."

"Great!" Kate said, then left the office and returned to the café. It was 8:45, and Bobbie was cleaning tables.

"I'm so sorry I'm late. Did the morning rush go okay?"

"Honey, we took care of it with no problems. What'd the mayor want?"

"He just wanted us to know if we needed anything, he'll help us out if he can."

"We could use him for cleaning tables, couldn't we? That'd be a hoot…the mayor cleaning tables."

Kate laughed. "Yeah, it would be a hoot. He's coming for lunch today at one o'clock. When he comes, I'll tell him we'll make a banana pudding if he wants to come on Tuesday. What do you think?"

"I think it'd be great. The mayor's coming to lunch! That'll be a treat. He's a charmer. Is he stuck on you?"

"Probably," Kate said without hesitation. She instantly thought about how she had answered Bobbie and asked herself why she didn't answer in a different way…like act empty-headed and pretend like she was completely unaware of any relationship between the mayor and her.

"But he's married."

"He's married, and I'm not stuck on him. Besides, I'm still grieving Marks…"

"I know, honey. You poor thing."

They continued cleaning tables, swept the floors, and then began cooking for lunch.

"Kate, we need to have something special for lunch since the mayor's coming."

Kate thought for a moment and said, "Well, he's Italian. Why don't we make spaghetti and meatballs?"

Bobbie clapped her hands and grinned. "Spaghetti and meatballs! Of course! We make the best spaghetti in the whole state, and Gill's meatballs are to die for!"

"Let's get to cooking," Kate said.

They prepared lunch, and the first customer appeared at 11:15 a.m., followed by another and another. It was show time.

Being part of the crew, Kate rushed to service the early patrons.

By noon, all the tables were occupied, and eight of the ten stools were being used as well.

Suddenly, Kate stopped. "Oh, my god!" she said. She walked hurriedly to the supplies shelf, got a piece of paper, scribbled "RESERVED" in tall letters on the bottom half of the paper, folded it so that the message would show, and placed it on the counter above the end stool and next to the walkway that led to the kitchen.

At a quarter of one, the mayor appeared.

Kate rushed to greet him and watched as his face developed a glow and a smile that covered his entire face.

"Mr. Mayor," Kate said loudly so that most of the patrons overheard her, "you look weary. Have you had a bad morning?"

The question seemed to jolt his thoughts because his face turned instantly to a frown. "It's Monday! The Budget Committee is wearing me ragged," he said and uttered a fakey laugh.

"You have to be careful, Mr. Mayor. You don't want to wind up in the hospital from being stressed out."

"A good meal should do the trick," he said and smiled.

"That it will, Mr. Mayor. Follow me. We have a seat for you," Kate said and walked to the stool that she had reserved for him.

"I can't wait till Friday," he whispered.

"It'll be something," Kate said. "Want a big glass of iced tea?"

"My favorite drink," the mayor said. "How's your day going?"

"It's been a pretty good day. We were busy all morning making something special for you."

"Really! I can't wait to see what it is. If you made it, I know it'll be great."

"Mr. Mayor, may I have a minute of your time?" a patron said.

The mayor turned to look at the woman who had interjected herself into the mayor's conversation with Kate. The smile on his face disappeared, and a frown appeared, but he said, "Of course."

Kate backed up slowly and walked into the kitchen. She couldn't believe her good fortune in being able to extract herself from the mayor's conversation. She sighed a breath of relief.

"Honey, are you okay?" Bobbie said.

"Oh, I'm fine. Just getting ready to take some spaghetti to the mayor. It's spaghetti today and banana pudding tomorrow. After we fill him with food this week, we're going to ask him for a new sidewalk in front of the café; we're going to ask him to install an awning to cover the sidewalk in front of the café; we're going to ask him to install a bench on either side of our front door and flowers to decorate the area; we're going to keep the mayor busy."

"I love it!" Bobbie said between bursts of laughter.

Bobbie's laughter was contagious, and Kate joined her, then picked up a dinner plate, and spooned a large serving of spaghetti over a boneless piece of chicken. She placed a serving of yellow squash and zucchini beside it, then picked up the plate and a bowl of mixed greens and took them to the mayor.

"My, my! That looks delicious! That's my favorite dish!" the mayor said.

"Hello, Mr. Mayor," a patron said as he walked by.

"You're a popular person," Kate said. "We hope you enjoy your lunch and please come at the same time tomorrow because we've planned a very special surprise, which we think you'll enjoy."

"I wouldn't miss it for the world...same time, same great company," the mayor said.

"I have some other customers I have to take care of, Mr. Mayor, but I'll be back," Kate said.

"Please do...as many times..."

"I will," Kate said before the mayor could finish his sentence, then she walked away to clear a table for a waiting customer. She picked up dirty dishes and walked by the mayor on the way to the kitchen.

"You can stop here and talk with me," the mayor said.

"I'll be back soon," Kate said in a low voice.

"Please do," the mayor said.

She continued into the kitchen, placed the dishes in the washer, and did as many mundane tasks as possible to use minutes before she went back into the dining room. Finally, she felt she had to return, so she walked out of the kitchen and stopped where the mayor sat.

"I thought you'd never get back," he said.

"I had several things I had to do. How's your lunch?"

"It's delicious…like I knew it would be. Tomorrow's another special surprise, you say?"

"A surprise that I believe will please your palate. It'll be something you'll remember forever," Kate said.

"I have a meeting to attend, so I can't stay any longer today, but you can bet I'll be back tomorrow," the mayor said.

"I'm sorry, you have to go."

"What's my damage today?" the mayor asked.

"I'll run a tab. Don't worry about it."

The mayor stood, lifted his arms, and extended them slightly forward to hug Kate but then withdrew them. "I wish I could," he said in a low voice.

"Later," Kate said.

"I'll see you tomorrow," the mayor said.

Kate smiled and said, "Until then."

The mayor hurried out, and Kate breathed deeply.

Bobbie walked by and said, "I thought he was gonna hug you, darlin.'"

"Shame on you! You think the most outlandish thoughts." Kate laughed. "Let's get to cleaning."

They went about their duties to wrap up the lunch period, which dragged on until two o'clock. Afterward, Kate and her staff had their own lunch and prepared for the dinner crowd.

At five-thirty, Kate's mother walked in. Kate rushed to her. "Mother, what a nice surprise. What are you doing here?"

"I've been shopping, my dear, and thought I'd stop and say hello to my first and only daughter. How's your day going?"

"It's going fine, Mother. We had the mayor for lunch, and that was a nice surprise. He sat on the stool next to the walkway to the kitchen, and I got to talk with him quite a bit."

"How charming. It's always fun to rub elbows with dignitaries, isn't it, honey?"

"Yes, it is, Mother."

"What time did the mayor drop in, honey?"

"Close to one. He only stayed about forty-five minutes today... had a meeting. He's coming tomorrow, and we're making our famous banana pudding for him."

"How delightful. I bet he likes his midday glass of tea too."

"He does."

"Banana pudding and tea. What a great combination!" Kate's mother said. "Are you going to make a big to-do when you serve the banana pudding?"

"You think we should?"

"By all means. You and the entire staff bring it out as if you're celebrating something special. Don't set it in front of the mayor. Bring it out and congregate behind him. Make a big presentation so the mayor will have to turn around and observe the festivities."

"What a great idea! So shall it be. You think of everything, Mother."

"When you're as old as I am, you'll have a few tricks up your sleeve too, honey."

Kate smiled. "Old you're not, Mother."

Sara leaned forward and kissed Kate on the cheek. "I'm off. By the way, I'm stopping by to see you about a quarter of one tomorrow. Do you need some help in the kitchen?"

"I can always use help in the kitchen."

"Good! Just let everyone know I'm coming."

"I'll tell everyone, and I'll remind them tomorrow morning."

"Good. I'll see you then."

"Goodbye, Mom," Kate said as she hugged her.

Sara left and Kate renewed her efforts to get ready for the dinner hour.

The afternoon and the dinner hour came and passed, then Kate went home at nine thirty. Once inside her home, she walked to her desk, pulled out her journal, and wrote:

October 21, 2002

Dear Journal:

Mothers are such angels. For example, my mother worries about my going to Atlanta to see a play; she worries that I'm alone at the café at night; she worries just to be worrying. She shouldn't worry so much because I've gotten used to handling things myself. Whatever she does though is alright with me. If she does worry, perhaps that is an indicator that all is not well. She's always been my rock, so I intend to keep her as close to my heart as possible.

Good night, Journal. I have another long day at work tomorrow.

Kate closed her journal and got ready for bed. When she was ready to turn in, she sashayed to the bed in a prissy motion. She smiled at herself, thinking how sexy she must look as she swayed from side to side in a rhythmic motion.

Kate's alarm sounded precisely at five. She reached over and turned it off, then leaned back to relax for a moment. Suddenly, she jerked upright. "I have to go! I have banana pudding to make," she said out loud.

She leaped out of bed, showered, and dressed. She wore her favorite dark green skirt and blouse. She accented it with a dark green necklace; it was made of dyed leather strips and held a dark green dime-sized ceramic ring. She had always thought of it as the ring of eternal love, a ring of power. Then she left home and drove to the café.

The air was chilly when she exited her car. She said, "Oooh" and walked as fast as she could into the café. Fall is here, she thought. Halloween's just around the corner, and winter's on its way.

"I hate winter," she said as she walked into the kitchen.

"Me, too," Bobbie said. "You're here early."

"Making banana pudding today for the mayor. Wanna help?"

"You betcha. Do you want me to get the wafers and bananas ready?"

"Yes, but don't cut the bananas until I get the mix ready. We don't want the little jewels to get dark. You can set the oven to 400 degrees too."

"Will do."

Kate layered the bottom of a large baking pan with vanilla wafers and prepared the pudding mix. "All right, girl, you can get those bananas cut and layer the bottom," she said.

"Yes, ma'am," Bobbie said as she grabbed a banana. She peeled it hurriedly, cut it into one-quarter inch pieces, placed them carefully on the wafers, then cut another and repeated the placement until she had covered all the wafers.

Kate poured the pudding onto the wafers and bananas. They then made a second layer and Kate covered the top with meringue. She waited ten minutes until the top was golden brown, then pulled the pan from the oven. "Whatta you think?" she asked Bobbie.

"That is the most bu…ti…ful pudding I've ever seen!"

Kate laughed.

The morning passed rapidly and soon the noon rush hour was well underway. Sara came at twelve-thirty and walked quickly to the kitchen. Along the way, several customers, having seen her during the span of twenty years of her tenure, spoke admiringly as she passed. Sara returned the pleasantries but maintained her pace.

Kate walked into the kitchen to get a salad for a customer.

"Hello, my daughter," Sara said as she tied an apron around her waist.

"Mother, what a surprise! You came to help us at the right time."

"Thank you, dear. I know all about this place."

Kate smiled, then picked up a salad and walked back into the dining room.

At 12:45, the mayor appeared, and again there was a small celebration at his being there. Kate guided him to the same stool he had occupied the day before; then Sara came out to greet him. She placed her arms loosely around his waist as he hugged her tightly, and when it became uncomfortable to her, she gently pulled away.

"Sara, you're as beautiful today as you were twenty years ago," he said.

"Well, thank you, Mr. Mayor. You've always been so gracious."

He chuckled. "Mayors have to be gracious."

Sara nodded. "Mr. Mayor, you look like you could go for a large glass of our famous tea."

"That I could...unsweet."

"Our pleasure," Sara said, hurrying back to the kitchen. She filled a glass half full of ice and filled the other half with tea. When she placed the glass in front of the mayor, she flashed him a smile. "Enjoy."

"Thank you, Sara. What a beautiful day this is turning out to be."

"You still look a little tired, Mr. Mayor," Kate said. "We've asked you so many times not to work so hard."

"I see him at all times of night," a man said. "Mr. Mayor, you're doing a great job," the man said and patted the mayor on the shoulder.

The mayor turned toward the speaker. "Thank you, Mr.–"

"Franks. Stan Franks."

"Thank you, Stan," he said as Sara stepped up to the counter.

"Mr. Mayor, how would you like an open-faced roast sandwich with gravy and potatoes?" Sara asked, leaning toward him.

"I was just thinking of that!"

"Salad?"

"Please...with oil and vinegar."

"Give me just a minute," Sara said, then walked back to the kitchen followed by Kate.

"Mother, is there anything I can do?"

"No, dear, you just go out and entertain the mayor." Sara kissed Kate on the cheek.

"You're such a great mother."

Sara smiled, then prepared the mayor's lunch and took it to him.

The mayor insisted Sara and Kate talk with him while he ate lunch, which they did, and they stood back when customers stopped by to say hello.

After he had finished eating, Kate said with much enthusiasm, "Mr. Mayor, do we have a surprise for you!"

"You do?"

"And I'll replenish the tea," Sara said, filling the glass to an inch from the top.

The mayor immediately gulped down leaving two inches of space at the top of the glass.

Back in the kitchen, Kate spooned out a double serving of banana pudding on a dinner plate, placed green garnish around the edge, and placed a round cover over the plate. She recruited Bobbie and Gill to walk in front of her. They walked back to the counter where the mayor sat and hurried behind him. As they walked, Kate shielded the plate so that the mayor couldn't see the contents, and then motioned Bobbie and Gill to stand beside her. When they were near her, she said, "Surprise!"

The mayor turned on the stool, and a large smile flashed across his face.

Customers nearby smiled and started clapping.

"My favorite, favorite, favorite dish!" he said in a booming voice.

As the celebration continued, Sara walked hurriedly from the kitchen wearing latex gloves and carrying a glass of tea that was filled two inches from the top of the glass. She placed it carefully on the counter where the mayor was seated, and then took the glass that she had filled earlier and placed it on a shelf underneath the counter on the opposite side. She then placed a straw in the glass that now rested in front of the mayor.

The celebration continued for another minute, and Kate said, "Mr. Mayor, it's time to start eating this special dish we made for you." She walked around the counter and placed the plate in front of him, as he simultaneously turned on the stool.

The mayor began eating. He took a long drink of tea using the straw and alternated between eating and drinking.

Five minutes passed. Suddenly, the mayor jerked forward on the stool. He jerked again and again. His face drained of any color, and his eyes were large and moving from side to side as if he had just encountered some horrific being. He jerked again, this time more violently.

Kate rushed to him and said, "Mr. Mayor, Is something wrong?"

His eyes turned to look at her but fluttered in their sockets; then, he jerked forward on the stool hitting his head on the counter. A gurgling sound came from his throat. He pitched backward and fell off the stool, his head and back striking the floor with a loud thud. The gurgling sound became louder as his chest heaved up and down as he struggled for air.

"Someone call nine-one-one!" Kate shouted. "The mayor's having a heart attack!"

The mayor's legs kicked forward, banged on the floor, and then recoiled.

"Hurry! Hurry!" Kate said.

Kate, Bobbie, Gill, and several customers crowded around the mayor looking down at him on the floor. Sara scanned the room once more, then she slipped on plastic gloves, took the mayor's tea and replaced it with the glass she had put under the counter earlier. She hurried to the kitchen holding the glass of tea in front of her. When she was out of sight of patrons and employees, she pulled a thermos from the bag she had brought to the café, opened it, and carefully poured the tea from the glass into it. She put a rubber cover over the empty glass, put it in a plastic bag, placed the bag in a second bag, and then put the double bag in a carrying case. She double-bagged her gloves and placed them inside the carrying case also. Holding her hands away from her body, she picked up a paper towel, poured a generous amount of soap on it, held it over the faucet, and washed her hands for one minute. She dried and repeated the process. She placed the paper towels in a plastic bag, put it in the carrying case, and hurried back to the counter.

"Move aside! Please move aside!" the man dressed in an emergency medical response uniform called out.

A second man pushing a gurney followed.

"This is the mayor!" the first man said.

"Must've had a terrible heart attack," Kate said. "It was awful. Do you have the equipment to check his heart?"

"We have to take him to the hospital. Let's go!" the man said and motioned to the second man.

They picked up the mayor, placed him on the gurney, rushed out of the café, loaded him into the ambulance, and sped away.

A man dressed in a suit walked hurriedly into the café.

"I'm Detective Martin," the man said, and then flipped open his badge. "What happened here?"

"I'm Kate. I'm the owner. He was having lunch and having a good time talking with us and the customers. We made a banana pudding especially for him, and he was so pleased and told us how much he appreciated our doing it. He didn't even get to have one bite of it…just fell off his stool and died. He must have had a massive heart attack," Kate said. "Detective Martin, we're in a state of shock. I think we'll close for the day."

"Detective, I'm Kate's mother. We were having a little celebration because the mayor loved banana pudding, and he's been under so much stress lately…at least, that's what we understood from him. Before he ate any of the banana pudding, he struggled for a moment, then fell off the stool. It was terrible."

"He complained about not feeling good yesterday," Kate said. "We asked him to slow down because he didn't look good."

"I want to take everything the mayor touched, what he was eating, what he was drinking," the detective said.

"I'll get everything together," Kate said.

"No, I'll get it. I don't want it touched by anyone, but I will take a tray if you have one."

"I have a shallow cardboard box," Kate said.

"That'll work."

Kate went to the kitchen, got a cardboard box, and walked back to the detective. "Will this work?"

"Yes, thanks," the detective said, then placed everything he assumed the mayor had touched including the plate, glass with tea, straw, fork, spoon, knife, napkin, and the salt and pepper shakers into the cardboard box. He picked up the box, then looked at each person near him. "Don't anyone leave town until I've finished with my investigation," he said. Then he took the box and left the café.

"We'll close down for the day," Kate said. "Bobbie, let's scrape the food off these dishes and throw them in the washer."

"Kate, I'm going home, honey. Come by after you close," Sara said.

"Okay, Mother."

Kate, Bobbie, and Gill cleaned the dishes; then Kate wrote on a sheet of paper that the café was closed for the day. She taped the note onto the front door, and then everyone left the café.

***

Kate drove to her mother's house and went inside.

"Honey, I'm burning some kitchen trash," Sara said. "Please come along."

Kate followed her mother out the back door, down the steps, then to a fire pit that was fifty feet away from the house and burning quite vigorously. Sara emptied some papers into the pit and said, "Step over there away from the fire, honey, and then bend down. I want to show you something about this fire pit."

Kate moved away from the pit, and then bent down.

Sara also bent down and opened her right hand, which held a folded piece of paper. She used her left hand to slowly unfold the paper. It read: "Don't talk about today. Someone may be listening and watching. There is no DNA. Everything is cleaned."

Kate looked at her mother and nodded slightly.

Sara lit the paper, moved her right hand close to the fire, opened it, and allowed the note to drift into the flames.

CHAPTER 9

Kate heard the soft chime that let her know the entrance door to the café was opening, so she picked up a guest check and walked out of the kitchen and into the dining area.

"Good morning. I'm looking for Kate Patterson," a man said, who had already made his way to a stool at the counter.

"I'm Kate."

"Hello, I'm Kenneth Cannon. I'm a reporter with the *Daily Reporter*. I have the first copy of today's breaking news. It says: 'Mayor Dies of Massive Heart Attack.' It took them a week to decide on it, but there it is. Heart disease, America's leading killer. So, Miss Patterson, now, no one can accuse you of food poisoning."

A noticeable hush settled instantly from the people overhearing the statement.

"Mr. Cannon," Kate said, "we don't serve poisoned food here, and I and all the people within hearing distance think your remark is callous and below what is expected of a professional reporter. Therefore, would you please leave?"

"But, I…"

"Now, Mr. Cannon!"

Kenneth looked at Kate for a moment. "Okay, I'm outta here." He began walking toward the entrance door, and suddenly turned and said, "It was a joke…a crudely stated joke maybe, but still a joke." The door slammed as he left.

"And good riddance!" Kate said.

"I think he caught your drift," Bobbie said.

"The very idea of being so catty."

Bobbie nodded. "At least we know now for sure what happened to the mayor. Some people might have thought he choked to death, so it's good we all know."

"Yeah, a heart attack," Kate said. "Let's get lunch ready."

They prepared food for lunch; then the lunch hour came and went. At three o'clock, a delivery man walked in carrying a dozen red roses.

Kate met the man and took the roses, which had a card that read: "For display on the small table near the entrance door."

The delivery man turned and began walking out, but Kate followed him. "Sir, sir, who was so thoughtful to send these?"

"I'm afraid it's confidential. I'm sorry."

Kate looked squarely at him. "Thank you anyway. Do you mind waiting for three or four minutes?"

"No, no, not at all."

Kate took the roses, walked behind the counter, put them in a trash can, and then walked back to the delivery man. "Tell your confidential customer that their roses are now decorating the dumpster," she said.

The man's eyes grew large as he looked at Kate, then he said, "I will. Yes, ma'am, I will," and walked out.

Having overheard Kate's conversation with the delivery man, Bobbie walked out of the kitchen. "Who do you think they're from, honey?" she asked Kate.

"The newspaper jerk, of course."

"Him?"

"Yep. Let's get ready for dinner."

They prepared dinner, and the dinner hour came and went. Afterward, Kate and the crew cleaned tables, washed the dishes, closed for the night, and went their separate ways to go home.

The next day, they did the same things over and over as if they were rehearsing for a great play. At three in the afternoon, however, a delivery man brought two dozen red roses, which Kate promptly took out to the dumpster.

On the following day, the delivery man said, "Ma'am, should I tell my customer?"

"Yep," she replied, smiling sweetly. "Please do."

At exactly three o'clock the following afternoon, a man holding two dozen roses walked slowly into the café. His head turned from one side to the other in robotic slow motion.

Bobbie walked to meet him.

"Is Miss Kate Patterson here today? I have a delivery for her."

"I'll get her for you," Bobbie said, and then hurried to the kitchen.

Almost instantly Kate emerged, then stopped short when she saw the man holding the roses. "Oh, it's you."

"Yes, it's me. I do hope you'll accept these as a small token of my regret for the poor choice of words I used about a very serious matter, one that affected you profoundly."

"And if I don't?" Kate said, and then looked toward the kitchen as a clatter interrupted her.

The entire kitchen staff stood in the kitchen doorway watching her.

"You shouldn't disappoint your staff," the man said, "and if you want to decorate the dumpster with these, I have ten more dozens in the car. I hope I don't have to go get them though."

Kate's eyes locked on his, and the seconds ticked by. After an awkward silence, Kate said," Sit them over there on the counter, in the middle, so everyone can see."

Hand clapping sounded instantly from the doorway to the kitchen. Just as quickly, the tight lines in the man's face relaxed and his cheeks moved to reveal a slight smile; then he walked over and placed the flowers in the center of the counter. He walked back to Kate. "I have tickets for *The Jersey Boys* Saturday night. It starts at eight, so what if I pick you up at five for dinner and the show?"

"What's the weather for Saturday night?"

"Clear, no rain, about sixty-five degrees."

"Five o'clock. Where do you want to meet?"

"I'll pick you up at your home."

"Do you want the address?"

"I have it. I'm in the newspaper business, you know."

"Oh. Well, I'll see you on Saturday. You're Ken Cannon?"

"Correct. Saturday it is," he said, and then turned and walked out of the café.

"You have a date, girl!" Bobbie yelled.

Kate walked to the doorway of the kitchen, a smile creeping across her face as she walked. "You people are so nosy," she said, and then hugged them as a group. She suddenly pulled away and said, "What am I going to wear?"

"A light green cocktail dress with matching jacket and three-inch, dark green heels," Bobbie said.

"How'd you become a fashion designer, girl? It's perfect!" Kate said. "Now, where do I find the perfect outfit?"

"Why don't you call Betty, your personal shopper?" Bobbie said.

Kate held both thumbs up and said, "You're two for two, girl." She walked to the front of the café and called Betty.

"Kate Patterson! I haven't heard from you in a long, long time! How are you?"

"I'm fine. Don't tell anyone, but I have a special date for Saturday night."

"Do you know what you're doin', honey?"

"We're having dinner and then going to see *The Jersey Boys.*"

"So you need a real sexy party dress?"

Kate laughed. "I'm not sure about the sexy part, but a party dress, yes. Maybe a light green with a jacket."

"I'll pick out some beautiful outfits just for you. Do you want to come to the store tonight to try them on?"

"Will eight o'clock be too late?"

"Eight o'clock will be just great. I'll see you then."

"Thanks, Betty. Thank you very much."

"Bye, Kate. See you soon."

Kate walked back to the kitchen. "Hey, you guys, can you take care of the ship tomorrow morning for a couple of hours?" she asked.

"Of course, honey," Bobbie said. "You go get your hair fixed and your nails done. We'll take care of everything."

"You know me well, Bobbie! Okay, I'll plan to be away from nine to eleven-thirty."

Kate and the crew prepared for the dinner hour and serviced the customers as they arrived. At twenty minutes after seven, Kate left the café, drove to the dress shop, met Betty and selected a dress, top, belt, and purse.

"You're going to look sensational! Let's go try these on," Betty said, and then picked up the dress and accessories.

Kate walked into the fitting room followed by Betty.

"I'll hang these here," Betty said. "Then I'll hang what you take off over here on these hangers."

Kate took off her slacks and blouse and gave them to Betty, who immediately took them and hung them on hangers.

"Here's the magnificent dress," Betty said.

Kate changed into it and looked at Betty.

"Stunning" Betty said. "And the fit is perfect! It hits you right at the knees. The top is snug but gives you room to breathe. What do you think?"

"I love it," Kate said, gushing.

"Let's see the top. Here you go," Betty said, and then gave the jacket to Kate.

Kate put it on and looked in the mirror again. "It's perfect," she said.

"And beautiful," Betty said. "You make the outfit beautiful."

"Okay, it's a winner, and I've kept you up really late."

"It's my pleasure. If you want to take those off, I'll put them in a nice bag while you finish dressing."

"Done," Kate said, and then pulled off the top and the dress and gave them to Betty. She finished dressing, paid for her new outfit, and then drove home. After parking her car, she retrieved her newly purchased clothes, hurried up the steps to her house, opened the door, and rushed in. She hung up her clothes and headed for her computer.

October 25, 2002

Dear Journal,

Dark clouds have obscured my travel for many past weeks, and I scowled and blamed other people, the weather, and any other thing that I could blame or that happened to be in the way. Today, however, a gigantic ray of sunshine drifted toward me and continued its progression until it engulfed my entire being. My spirit was lifted, but it was like a crippled man learning to walk. It grew in intensity though, and it reached a level that I felt as if I had drunk from the fountain of youth.

I feel as if my spirit and basket of emotions have been rekindled. I am optimistic that my journey along the path of my existence will become joyous; flowers will spring up; birds will sing; bright rays of sunshine will light the way.

I must sign off. I have new clothes to try on and model in front of my full-length mirror.

"I'm back," Kate said, and then she took off her clothes and put on the new party dress and jacket. She put on the three-inch heels, picked up the purse, held it in her left hand waist-high, and then walked to the mirror. A trim figure with medium red hair elevated by the heels to five-foot-nine with noticeably protruding butt and breasts enveloped in the soft green dress stared back at her. "Wow!" she said. "I'd want me."

Feeling she would have trouble going to sleep, she took two Tylenol PM capsules, brushed her teeth, and went to bed.

***

The next morning Kate took a shower, hurried out of her home, and drove to Melba's hair salon. She parked and then walked briskly into the shop.

"Good morning, beautiful!" Melba said.

"Good morning, my savior. Thank you for being sweet and taking time to make me better."

"Make you better? After I get that red hair shampooed and styled, you're going to be glam-a-rus! Carrie will be here in about five minutes to make your nails beautiful. What time is the big date?"

"I have to be ready at five."

"Are you leaving from the café, home, or somewhere else?"

"Home."

"Good! Why don't you come back at three-thirty? I'll tidy your hair, and Carrie will dress up your nails? At four, you'll be Miss America!"

"You're a sweetheart!" Kate said and then hugged Melba.

Melba finished Kate's hair, and Carrie completed her nails. "Thank you Melba, and thank you Carrie," Kate said, and then she paid them, walked out of the shop, got in her car, and drove to the café.

***

It was ten-thirty, and the café was empty...a rare moment after breakfast and just before lunch.

Kate walked to the kitchen. The noise of her steps caused everyone to turn and look.

"Wow!" Bobbie said.

The exclamation was repeated by everyone in the kitchen.

Kate smiled. "All of you are blind," she said.

"Oh, no, we're not!" Bobbie said. "You look terrific."

"Well, thank you," Kate said as a noticeable tint of red sprang into her cheeks. "You haven't seen the green dress, but I'll take a picture if anyone's interested."

"You'd better," Bobbie said.

"Yeah," Sharon and Gill said in unison.

Everyone returned to their duties, and Kate worked through the lunch hour performing her tasks mainly by rote. Her usual focus on duties was obscured by her thoughts of the afternoon…what time to leave the café? Should she go by Melba's shop to get her nails freshened…how much time to shower and get dressed? Will she be overdressed, especially for the first date?

She looked for different chores to keep her busy and move the clock ahead. She hadn't experienced the emotions she was feeling for many months. The more she rushed to perform a job, the slower the clock moved. The more anxious she felt the faster her heart beat. Finally, though, the clock rolled to ten after three, and Kate left the café, drove to Melba's, and hurried inside.

"Come on in here, girl! Give us twenty minutes, and we'll get you outta here," Melba said. "Carrie, honey, come and check Kate's nails 'cause she's out on the town tonight."

Kate smiled. "You do so much for me," she said. "I thought the clock was stuck today. I haven't had a date in a long time, and I'm a little anxious."

Melba and Carrie laughed.

"May I make a confession to the two of you?" Kate said.

"Absolutely, honey," Melba said.

"I…I feel like I'm sixteen."

"Honey, if you feel like you're sixteen, you got the magic," Melba said. "When we get finished with you, every man in Nashville's gonna want a piece of you."

Kate laughed then used her index finger to tap Melba on the chin. "You!" she said.

Melba and Carrie finished their work, then Kate left the shop, drove home, and hurried inside. "I'll write you later, Journal," she said as she walked past the desk that held her journal. She undressed, brushed her teeth, took a quick shower, massaged moisturizing lotion into her cheeks and forehead, applied a light eye shadow, put on a light green bra and underwear, donned the party dress, and—last but not least—applied a light red lipstick. She checked her face and hair, and then sat down and pulled on her heels. She stood up and twisted slowly from side to side in front of the full-length mirror. "You do look pretty. In fact, you look glamorous and sexy," she told her reflection.

The clock finally rolled to five, and instantly the doorbell rang.

Kate hesitated for a moment, and then walked over and opened the door.

"Wow!"

"Thank you," Kate said as a smile softened the features of her face. "Do you go by Ken, Kenneth, or something else?"

"My friends call me Ken. You're welcome to call me Ken; you're welcome to call me Kenneth: you're welcome to call me Bozo if you like…whatever strikes your fancy."

Kate laughed. "Well, since we're having this big date, I'll call you Ken."

Ken's mouth opened revealing his extremely white teeth. He was tall, standing at six feet, two inches. He had dark brown hair, and his face was tanned from being on assignments with the newspaper. He had very noticeable dimples, which made it seem as if he was constantly smiling. It was difficult to know when he was actually smiling.

"Maybe this big date will create a friendship so that a bouquet of flowers will be a token of friendship rather than one of apology," he said, grinning.

They both laughed.

"Shall we?" Ken said.

"Let's," Kate said, then stepped out onto the walkway to the front entrance and reached to close the door.

"I'll get it," Ken said.

"Oh."

Ken pulled the door shut, pulled on it to make sure it was locked, and then stepped beside Kate. "Let's go for it," he said.

They walked to Ken's car, and he hurried to the passenger side, opened the door, waited for Kate to get in, and closed the door.

Even in the dusk, Kate could see how clean the car was, how clean it smelled, and she made a mental note of her impression.

Ken drove out of Kate's community, onto the interstate, into the heart of the city, then pulled into the valet area of a restaurant.

"We're going here?"

"We are."

"This is a five-star restaurant," Kate said.

"I know. I hope you enjoy it."

"I'm sure I will. I've never been here."

Two valet attendants opened the driver's door and the passenger's door simultaneously. Ken and Kate stepped out and went into the restaurant where a hostess seated them and presented a menu. Ken said, "Do you mind if I order for you?"

The question was like a gut punch to Kate's independence, and she thought about it and how to answer it, but finally said, "Okay, sure."

Ken ordered a bottle of expensive champagne, and identical orders of filet mignon, baked potato, and a salad. "I'm so glad you accepted my invitation to come out tonight. This has been a rough week," he told Kate. He began detailing the stories that were associated with the assignments he had been working at the newspaper. Then, he related in detail some stories that had a peculiar twist, some that had a comedic twist, and some that were serious.

"Interesting," Kate said.

They finished the meal then took a shuttle van to the theater, saw the Jersey Boys, took the shuttle back to the restaurant, had coffee; then Ken took Kate home.

"I had a good time," Kate said. "Thank you. The Jersey Boys were fantastic."

"I'm happy you enjoyed it. That gives me the impetus to ask if you would accompany me to the football game tomorrow. I have great seats. The game starts at noon, and the weather is supposed to be perfect. How about it?"

Kate thought for a moment, then said, "Sure. I don't know much about how the team's doing, so you'll have to fill me in."

"Oh, no problem. We'll have a great time. So, pick you up at nine-thirty?"

"That early?"

"Oh, yes, the traffic's horrendous, and we'll need a snack before the game."

"Okay, nine-thirty," Kate said, then she moved over and lightly kissed him on the cheek.

He smiled and looked into her eyes. "I'll see you tomorrow morning."

"Good night," Kate said and went into her home. She walked to her desk and pulled out her journal, selected a pen, and wrote:

Saturday, October 26, 2002

Dear Journal,

I stepped out and drove to the moon tonight. The trip was interesting, but the surface of the moon was intriguing. Because it was new and different, I'm not sure that I grasped the meaning of it all. I certainly didn't understand the ingredients of the material that dominated the scenery, but days are ahead and discoveries are ahead. I'm in no hurry, however, to formulate a nugget of intelligence that will reveal all the truths of the material.

I must sign off. I have a football game to attend tomorrow, and I have no idea what to wear, so I'll be doing some research on the computer tonight.

Kate closed her journal, turned to her computer, and Googled: *What do women wear to NFL football games?*

Several topics appeared, and Kate read a few sentences of a few articles. She decided to wear brown cotton jeans, brown sneakers, a white over blouse with a dark beige tee, and a dark beige windbreaker. She then walked to her closet, pulled out the items, and then carefully hung them on a hanger that was mounted on the closet door. She got ready for bed and set her alarm for six-thirty.

***

On Saturday, Kate got up, showered, brushed and combed her hair, applied makeup, checked her fingernails and eyelashes. When she looked at the clock, it was 8 a.m. She pulled on a robe, walked to her computer, and Googled *Football Terminology*. She read paragraphs from several articles, then typed *Football Positions*. She knew the role of quarterback, but she spent several minutes reading about other positions. When the clock rolled to eight-thirty, she said, "Time for game of the day," then changed into the clothes she had selected earlier. She looked into the mirror twice to check her face and decided that she was as ready as she could be. The clock showed that it was nine-fifteen, so she had fifteen minutes to wait.

Finally, the doorbell rang precisely at nine-thirty. She opened the door and saw that Ken was wearing jeans and a blue pullover sweater.

"Ready for some football?" he asked.

"I'm ready. Am I overdressed?"

"Not at all. You look great. You can always call me if you have a question about anything. Being in the work I'm in, I have to stay up to snuff on fashion, fads, that kind of stuff."

"Oh, okay."

When they arrived at the stadium, Ken drove to the parking area. "I have a special parking pass," he said. "We just walk across the street there and go right in."

"That's great! This is one busy place."

"Yeah, I love football. Fact is, I love most sports, and that's a good thing because we have to stay on top of all the events in the newspaper. Here, I'll get the door for you," he said as they exited the car.

"Thank you. I think I'm going to like this."

"I'm going to do everything possible to make sure you do. That way, we can have some more big dates."

They laughed then walked into the stadium, ate a sandwich, and found their seats, which Ken pointed out were Club Level seats and cost a lot of money.

The game started and every time Ken would yell, Kate would yell. Every time he would groan, she would groan.

When the game ended, Ken hurried her to the car to beat the crowd; then he drove her home. "You were a real topper today," he said.

"Well, I had a good time," she said, and then leaned over and kissed him on the cheek before hopping out of the car and going inside.

October 27, 2002...Sunday

Dear Journal,

I'm back. It seems I've been riding a comet. Just in case though, I'm holding onto the donkey as we walk up the mountain. I sort of feel like there's gold in Them Thar Hills. I'll keep you informed. Signing off.

CHAPTER 10

The next three weeks were crammed full of activity. Ken seemed to have tickets for every event, regardless of how scarce tickets were. They went to football games, musical events, plays, and dinner cruises on the Cumberland River.

After the third week, Ken proposed they have sex. Kate had thought about it several days earlier and wondered to herself if she was not clicking with him. When he made the proposal, she said, "You know, we're compatible in so many ways, we might as well find out if we're compatible with that. Your house or mine?"

"Let's try mine."

They went to his house, got comfortable, and had sex. There was no preparing each other to do it because each one immediately felt the passion. Afterward, each one told the other that it was the greatest thing that had ever happened to them. It was so good that Ken wanted to do it every night. Kate was just as thrilled and agreed without hesitation.

For the three following weeks, they went to events and had daily sex. On Thursday of the fourth week, Ken informed Kate that he had just gotten an assignment that required he leave that night and would be out of town for the entire weekend. Both of them expressed their disappointment and sadness at the prospect of being apart and vowed they would hold each other in their hearts. Kate hoped she might be able to leave the café and say goodbye to Ken, but it didn't happen; the café was extremely busy.

Ken left a message at six o'clock and said he was leaving, that he loved her, and he would see her either late Sunday night or early Monday morning.

At seven o'clock, Kate's mother called.

"Yes, Mother."

"Honey, will you come and see me after you close?"

"It may be late."

"I don't work, honey, and I don't have a hot date."

"Okay, Mom, I'll see you later."

Kate and the crew finished cleaning at eight-thirty, and then closed for the night.

Kate drove to her mother's house, walked up the steps, and knocked on the door. The door opened immediately, and her mother smiled and ushered her in.

"Mother, if I look shocked, maybe I am. Why are you being so nice?"

"Why, honey, I'm always nice. Would you like a glass of wine?"

"A glass of wine? Okay, now I really know. You're someone pretending to be my mother."

Sara laughed, and then poured two fingers into a glass and gave it to Kate.

Kate sipped the wine. "Okay, what's up?"

"Honey, I just wanted to see you. How are you and Ken getting along?"

Kate laughed. "Now, I know. You're wondering if we're seeing each other every day, if we're happy, if we're getting along without conflict, and if we've had sex. I know you like the back of my hand. You want to know everything your daughter—even though she's grown up—is doing."

"Well, maybe some of those things, but not all of them. After all, I'm your mother."

"It's like a storybook romance, Mother. We're so compatible and so happy together. Ken has front row tickets to every event that comes to town. We're out going places, eating at the finest restaurants, and just being happy together. Most people would give their eye teeth to do all the things we've done and are doing. Like I said, it's like a story-book…a wonderful dream."

"There's something you should know that I just learned today."

"Learned? Learned what, Mother?"

"I met Diane today…Diane who works in the County Clerk's office. She knows Ken, and her office knows all about the legal stuff that's going on."

"So what's that got to do with Ken?"

"Well, it seems that Ken took out a second mortgage on his home just shortly after he started seeing you. He cashed out about fifty thousand, but he hasn't been making his payments on the loan. He's about to lose his house."

"What!"

"It's true, honey."

"You mean he's been wining and dining me on borrowed money?"

"I'm afraid so."

"He mortgaged his house and blew the money just to go places with me?"

"It would appear so."

"Ignorant! Stupid! All those things we went to weren't at the top of my list. I mean, we could have just had a sandwich, taken a walk in the park, or just stayed home and watched TV."

"I'm sorry, honey."

"Well, I'm going to confront him and let him know what an asshole he's been."

"I hope he takes it well."

"Well or not well, he's going to get an ear full. He's out of town this weekend, but I can wait until Monday, and Monday's coming. I'm going, Mother. I have a lot to do at home."

"Okay, dear. I'm here, and I'll always be here. Call me if you need me."

Kate drove home, got out of her car, walked into her house, and straight to her desk. She pulled out her journal and wrote:

November 29, 2002...Friday

Dear Journal,

Over the past days and weeks, I have enjoyed the most happiness and bliss of my lifetime. Sometimes, I reveled in my good fortune. I lay awake at night and smiled at my wonderful thoughts. Tonight, my bubble burst. I now have the worst feeling in my gut.

I allowed my clouded emotions overrule good judgment. I allowed a good friend to be misguided in his financial dealings. But I also have now discovered that my good friend lacks wisdom and is weak in his mental planning. In that regard, I must confront him and reassure myself that I have made a correct determination about his character.

I will close for now, but I'm sure I will have more to tell you on another day...soon.

Although it was ten o'clock, it was early for Kate to go to bed, but she felt anxious and wanted the night to be over, the next day to be over, the weekend to be over, and Monday to arrive. By habit, she did all the things she usually did to get ready for bed, then climbed into bed. She set the alarm for five o'clock, and then told herself that if she could go to sleep, the time would fly by, and the morning would come. She fell asleep rather quickly, but she was restless and tossed the entire night.

She awakened before the alarm sounded and felt physically and mentally drained due to inadequate rest, but she got ready for work, drove to the café, put in her time, and then repeated the same thing on Saturday. She stayed busy Sunday by cleaning the café and then went home and vacuumed and washed clothes. Later that night, she selected her clothing for Monday, and then read until she fell asleep.

Kate awakened at four-thirty Monday morning, visited the bathroom, washed her hands, brushed her teeth, and then went to the kitchen and made coffee.

At five o'clock, her cell phone rang. She looked at the display and saw that it was Ken, so she answered, "Good morning, sweetheart! Welcome back!"

"I've missed you! I couldn't call over the weekend because I was involved in a confidential matter."

"I thought you were. That's why I didn't try to call you."

"What if I come over now?"

"Darling, let's wait until tonight, say about nine o'clock at my house."

"That's an eternity!"

"I know. I know, but it'll be worth it. We'll have the whole night."

"Okay. Okay. Tonight at nine o'clock at your place. I love you."

"I love you. See you tonight," Kate said, and then hung up.

She got ready for work then drove to the café. As usual, the day flew by and at eight-thirty, she finally drew a long breath.

"I hate to go," she said to Bobbie. "Do you mind locking up?"

"No, honey, you go on ahead. We'll take care of everything."

"You're a blessing," Kate said, and then rushed out the door and drove home. She arrived five minutes before nine. Ken was already there.

They hurried toward each other, and then embraced in the driveway.

"God, I've missed you," Ken said.

"I've missed you, too, sweetheart. I thought Monday would never get here."

"Let's go in and get reacquainted."

"Let's, but I want to take a minute and talk with you about something," Kate said, and then took his hand as they walked up the steps and into the house.

"Can't it wait just a little while?" Ken asked.

"It'll just take a minute, sweetie."

"Okay. Okay, but I haven't seen you in four days. It's been agony. I mean, I've just about gone crazy. So here we are together, and you want one minute. Let the minute begin."

"You've been wonderful these past weeks. You've taken me to every sports event, every concert, every play, and every other event that was happening. We went to the mountains, to the theater in Atlanta, to New York shows, to a concert in St. Louis, to Las Vegas, and many, many other places. We've eaten at the finest restaurants; we've had catered picnics in parks; we've done so many wonderful things…"

"Okay, this sounds like you're leading up to something, and I'm beginning to feel a little apprehensive."

"No! No! Nothing bad! Nothing bad!"

"But you're getting to something?"

"It's just that all the things we've done have cost a lot of money."

"Well, it does cost some money to do things, but I have it, and I'm so happy to share it with you."

"But, sweetheart, it is much more expensive than an average person makes."

"Kate, you're getting at something. What is it?" Ken seemed agitated.

"Yes, I suppose I'm getting at something, and it's touchy. It's about money, and that's very touchy. I just heard over the weekend that your mortgage is behind…well, two mortgages."

"What? Where did you hear that?" Ken said, raising his voice.

"Wait! Wait! I don't want to upset you. I was just concerned and want to work with you if there's a problem. I care for you, and if you have a problem, it concerns me too."

"I don't think you heard me! Who said I'm having financial problems?" Ken said, his eyes glaring and his jaw set.

Kate looked back at him and suddenly found herself assessing Ken's attitude. "It was just…just two customers talking. I just happened to overhear them. I don't know their names. They're not regulars."

"That's bullshit! You're feeding me a line of bullshit! Of course, you know who they are!" Ken said, his voice sounding thick and loud. He grabbed Kate's arm and said loudly, "What are their names?"

Kate jerked back and tried to release Ken's grip, but he held tight. "Ken, you're squeezing my arm," she said and again attempted to pull free, but Ken held her arm firmly. She tugged again and then slapped his face with her other hand.

"You lyin' witch," he said, his words terse and coming forcibly through clenched teeth. "How about this?" he said then punched her in the face with a closed fist while continuing to hold her arm with his other hand.

Kate reeled backward, and her left eye immediately turned red and closed.

"And this," he said, and then punched her again.

Blood gushed from her nose.

He grabbed her arm with both his hands and slung her viciously across the room. Her body hurtled away from Ken, her hands flailing and thrashing crazily in the air, and then she crashed into the wall. She stood upright for a moment, and then collapsed.

Ken walked across the room, reached down, and grabbed a handful of Kate's hair with his left hand; then he backhanded her face with his other hand. "Stay outta my business," he said, and then released the grip on her hair and stormed out of the house.

Kate lay on the floor without movement for about twenty minutes. Finally, she lifted her head and moaned; pain radiated from her back and left side. Her right eye opened slightly, and she looked across the room through her squinting eye. The effort was in slow motion, and everything looked cloudy. After five minutes of squinting and forcibly making herself look at the floor one foot at a time, her spirits lifted slightly when she spotted her purse. She attempted to crawl, but the pain was so severe that she had to stop. Her side throbbed, so she lay still and gave up the thought of calling for help.

Twenty more minutes passed, then a faint noise came from across the room. Kate heard it, but she couldn't recognize it, and she couldn't do anything about it anyway. Five seconds later, she heard it again. A third sound came at the same interval as the first and second. Then there was silence. Kate lapsed in and out of consciousness.

Ten minutes passed, then the front door opened. Footsteps approached slowly, then became more rapid.

"Kate! Kate! Wha…?"

"Moth…"

"Kate, you're hurt! I'm calling an ambulance!" Sara said, then called 911 and told the operator to send an ambulance immediately. She hurried to the kitchen sink, ran cold water on a towel, wrung out the excess water, then returned to Kate and placed it gently on her forehead. "Help is on the way, honey. Whatever happened to you we're going to get you well. After that, we're going to find out who and why, and we're going to fix that too."

"Uh…"

"Don't try to talk, sweetheart. Ah, there's the siren. Help's almost here."

Seconds ticked by, and the siren became louder and louder until it was in front of Kate's house. Then it stopped, and rapid knocks sounded on the front door.

Sara rushed across the room and opened the door.

"Is there a problem here, ma'am?" a tall man said. He wore a uniform with EMT written on the upper left side of his shirt.

"Yes! Yes! My daughter! She had a terrible accident. Over here." Sara walked quickly back across the room.

The man in uniform followed. He looked down at Kate. "Dwayne, bring the gurney," he said, talking into a microphone attached to his shirt. He looked at Sara, and said, "Ma'am, we're going to take her to the hospital."

CHAPTER 11

"Honey, let's get you out of here," Sara said.

"I'm ready. I'm packed. I was ready two days ago," Kate said.

"A nurse has to roll you out exactly at eleven o'clock. I'll go pull the car up. Now, you stay right here. Okay?"

"Okay, Mother. There aren't many places I can go from here. Let's hurry. I've been keeping this bed company for four days now."

"I'll be back in a flash. I'll take your bags." Sara picked up Kate's suitcase and purse and walked out.

"Kate Patterson?"

"Yes, Martha, it's me, Kate. You've known me for twenty years. My birthdate is June 15, 1975. If you have any compassion, you'll pull that chair over here and get me out of here."

"Kate, you've got three cracked ribs, a jaw that's a hair away from being crushed, a black eye, and god knows what else. You're lucky to be in a great hospital that gives you the best of care."

"Martha, you sold me already! Get me out of here!"

"Climb in my chair."

Kate moved quickly, but the pain in her side felt like a knife. She grabbed her side and moaned.

"I told you, you shouldn't be going home yet!"

"Ohhhh," Kate said in an angry tone. "It made you feel good to remind me, didn't it?"

"It's good for you, I'm not the doctor. I would have kept you another five days. You don't need to be out of the hospital banged up as you are."

"I hope you become a doctor. I really do, but today it's just you and me. If you get me out of here really fast, I'll give you two free dinners at the cafe."

"Well, in that case, hang on girl 'cause we're goin' to take all turns on one wheel!"

"Atta, girl."

Martha was true to her word. She pushed the wheelchair with Kate quickly down the corridors of the hospital. People walking in the hallways would step aside as the wheelchair zoomed by.

Kate smiled. She remembered watching the scenery from a fast-speed train she once took, only this time, it was people clinging to the walls.

When the double doors opened, Martha rolled her out onto the sidewalk. Sara was parked alongside the walkway and waiting; she opened the passenger door.

"I'm going to hold you under the armpits until you get in the car," Martha said.

"I'm in. Martha, thank you. You are really a jewel. All those bad things I said about you were in jest. See you in a couple of weeks."

"Take care of yourself," Martha said. "Call me or come back here if you have a problem."

"I'll be fine," Kate said, then turned to look at her mother, who had gotten back into the driver's seat. "Let's go, Mother."

"We're off," Sara said.

They drove away from the hospital and onto the street that led to the interstate, which they took for a total of ten miles; then they took the street to Kate's home.

"Are you okay, honey?"

"I'm fine, Mother."

"I hope you let me take care of that son of a bitch. I'll do it real gentle."

"No, Mother, I'll take care of it. I've thought about it every hour, every minute, every second for several days now, and it's not going to be gentle."

"Just be careful," Sara said, and then guided the car onto the interstate.

"Any problems at the café?"

"No, I'm just enjoying seeing some old customers."

"Any scuttlebutt about me?"

"No, I'm just telling everyone that you had a gall bladder attack, and the doctor restricted you to bed for a week."

"A gall bladder attack!"

"Well, honey, it's all I could think of right at the moment."

"Mom, you could have told them I fell off a roof, or two bears attacked me, or a bus hit me, but a gall bladder attack? That makes me look like a sickie! I mean, old people have gall bladder attacks!"

"Well, honey, I'll go back and tell them I made a mistake…that you really had brain surgery."

Kate looked at her mother for a moment, and then both of them burst out laughing.

"Here we are, home again. I came over here before I came to the hospital and made you two sandwiches, a bowl of fruit, and a whole pitcher of fresh tea. I also opened out the recliner so you can rest, eat, and watch TV. I'll go to the café until six, and then I'll come and spend the night with my beautiful daughter. Did I forget anything?"

Kate looked at her mother for a moment and said, "Mother, sometimes you really floor me. I mean, you're the greatest mother any daughter could wish for. Thank you."

"And you love your mother?"

"Any mother…"

"And you love your mother?"

"Yes, I love my mother. There, now you know."

Sara smiled. "I knew it. I knew it all along."

"Okay, Mother, let's get your daughter in the house."

"Stay put. I'll be around to help you up the steps."

"Let me get out by myself, Mother. I need to see if I can get up the steps without any help."

"Okay, honey. I'll be right behind you."

"I'll get it," Sara said quickly then opened the front door.

Once Sara had helped Kate up the steps, she hurried to open the front door.

Kate looked in and said, "This brings back very bad vibes."

"I know it does, honey. I changed the furniture around as much as I could manage. I thought that might help."

"Thank you, Mother. I'm a big girl. I'll make it. Besides, it'll help me carve into my brain what happened here. It'll provide even more impetus for the days ahead."

"Let me help you to your chair."

"Thank you. I am a little pooped." Kate took her mother's hand, walked slowly to the recliner, and lowered herself to sit down. "I'm in," she said. "You're a wonderful mother, but you have to be tired too. Go take care of your personal things. I'll be okay. Oh, before you go, will you please bring my journal and a pen? They're in my top desk drawer."

"Sure, honey," Sara said, and then got the journal and pen and gave them to Kate.

"Thank you."

"Call me if you need anything," Sara said, drawing out the word, "anything."

"I will."

When Sara had left, Kate opened her Journal and wrote:

October 28, 2010

Dear Journal,

I've missed you for almost a week now. I've been camping out at the local hospital. Seems one of my acquaintances and I had a disagreement. A man and a woman disagreeing sometimes have an unhappy ending. The man is usually stronger, you know…not in the head but in the biceps.

I love Mother, but I am in desperate need of warmth in my life from an individual that is not in my bloodline. I want to frolic on a hillside, be lovingly thrown down in the sagebrush, roll in it, and look at the shape of the clouds and imagine all kinds of animals and objects. I want life.

I'm going to sign off, but I'll be back to report when I have some better news.

Kate placed the journal and the pen on the floor next to her chair. She settled back and said, "Okay, it's time to start healing."

***

For the next three days, a nurse came by to perform physical therapy and check on Kate's progress. Every passing day, Kate felt stronger and the pain lessened.

On the fourth day, her phone rang. She looked at the display and saw that it was Ken. Her heart raced, and she felt uncertain and confused. She wasn't prepared for the call just yet, but she said, "Hello."

"Kate, thank god you answered. I've been so worried, and it's all my fault. I dialed your number at least twenty times but wouldn't let the phone ring. I finally got the nerve to actually call you today. Am I too late? I mean, am I skating on thin ice…or no ice?"

A thousand thoughts raced through Kate's head. Finally, she said, "Ken, I'm not able to talk right now. I'll call you tomorrow."

"Tomorrow? Okay, tomorrow. It'll be a long twenty-four hours, but if I'm able to talk with you, I'll make it."

Kate hung up without saying anything. Thoughts ran rampant, but suddenly, she had a plan. She thought about doing some research on the computer but decided against it because it was traceable. She got up from her chair, walked to the bathroom, and looked into the mirror. A lot noticeable, she thought; so, she applied a coat of makeup around her eyes and over her cheeks. Then she applied another round. She looked again and was somewhat satisfied, and then she brushed over the makeup to blend it. She brushed her hair and said, "At least my red hair's still beautiful. I'm going shopping."

She pulled on a sweater; the leaves were falling and the days were cooler now. When she got in her car and started driving, she felt strange. It felt strange driving, seeing people, looking at storefronts she knew so well.

At the grocery store, she walked down the aisle that had items for barbecuing. A woman approached her. "Hi, Kate, how are you feeling?"

"Oh, Josey," Kate said, and then paused because she was completely caught off guard by meeting Josey, a customer. "I'm fine," she said after the awkward moment. "How are you and the family?"

"We're fine. Daniel's doing great in school, and Bubba's the same ol' Bubba working at his shop. You're out shopping for the café?"

Kate laughed. "Yes, I'm always shopping for the café. I wouldn't know what to do if I couldn't come to the grocery store."

Josey laughed. "Well, take care now. I'll see you at the café."

"Thank you. I'll see you there."

Josey walked away and then disappeared into another aisle.

"This was not the right time for Josey," Kate said in a low voice. She looked at the lighter fluid and wasn't too excited about it for some unconscious reason, so she left the store and walked to the pet store. Why? She didn't know. She walked casually down the aisles. Suddenly, she stopped. "Flea & Tick Spray," the label read. "Warning, highly flammable. Fumes are combustible. Do not use around open flames."

"Ah!" She picked up three of the spray bottles, took them to the checkout counter, paid for them with cash, and then left the store. Next, she drove to the mall. During the drive, she debated with herself about how to purchase handcuffs and several pieces of rope. She could order them from the internet, but it would take too much time for delivery and would be traceable. She could pay someone to buy them for her at the Adult Toy Store, but she would create a traceable link there also. Finally, she decided to purchase them herself, so she went to the Adult Toy Store and purchased the items. She returned to her car and drove home. When she'd put her packages away, she went to her desk and began writing in her journal.

November 2, 2010

Dear Journal,

I continue to search for someone to love me. I am a good person. I'm pretty, and I have a good heart. I consider other people's feelings. I share myself with a partner, and I think I'm good at it. In a partnership, I would pull my load; I would be considerate; I would give my whole being, all my love.

But, Journal, I do know when I don't have love. I do know when I'm at the top of the mountain and when I look down, I don't see anything. I do know that when I have walked through the wilderness and suffered cuts and scrapes and bruises in my quest for love, then I must return to the place where the thorns grow and purge them from the forest. The big question though is what instrument is used in performing the purge? It's a question that each person on this planet must solve in order to preserve their identity and survival. The whole affair of living is complicated, isn't it, Journal? I'll sign off now. Later.

After having something to eat and resting, Kate assembled the items she had purchased at the pet store and the Adult Toy Store. She pulled out four pieces of six-foot nylon rope. She took one piece, looked at it, and then rolled it back and forth. This was something she never had done, and she was in a quandary as to how it should be done. Finally, she took one end of one rope, turned it so that it formed a loop, and then took the same end and wrapped it around the bottom of the loop and tied it to make a slipknot.

She studied the rope trying to determine what the next step should be. After a minute, she took the opposite end of the rope and slipped it through the slipknot, placed one foot into the circle of the rope she had made, and pulled it taut enclosing her foot. She smiled, realizing she had solved one piece of the puzzle. The second problem would be how to tie off the end without the slipknot. Suddenly, she remembered a piece of furniture at Ken's house. She smiled.

She needed to become familiar with the handcuffs too. She pulled them from the package, placed them around a doorknob, locked them, and then unlocked them. She took them off the doorknob and took a mental inventory of what she had done; then, she felt she was prepared.

She lay down on the bed to rest again. Instead, she fell asleep.

Two hours passed, and she awakened. Everything was foggy, but she finally gained her composure. "The time has come," she said, and then dialed Ken's number.

"Kate, I'm so happy to hear from you. I haven't slept since we talked yesterday. Could we get together and talk about things over a cup of coffee?"

"I think that would be nice," Kate said, "but I was thinking about something both of us enjoyed in the past."

"And..."

"Ken, I've missed our sexual activity. Have you?"

"Oh, my god, I have!"

"Would you be agreeable to some kinky sex?"

"Kinky?"

"Yes, I'll be the instigator. What do you think?"

"I love it! When and where?"

"Tomorrow at your house. What about after you get off work? Say six-thirty?"

"Yes, yes! I'll be counting the seconds until then!"

"Good! I'll see you there."

"I'll be waiting."

Kate clicked off her telephone. *I have some packing to do,* she thought.

She walked to her bedroom closet and selected a twenty-four-inch wide by sixteen-inch-tall tote bag, then walked back to her desk and picked up the handcuffs and placed them in the bag. She picked up the ropes, made a slipknot on one end of each of them, folded each one into an odd-sized ball, and then placed them one by one in the bag. She placed the three spray bottles of flea and tick spray in the bag, then walked to the kitchen, got a box of matches, and placed them in the bag. "Just in case modern technology doesn't work out," she said. She walked to the fireplace mantle in the living room, got the lighter, which would extend to three feet, and placed it in the bag.

As an afterthought, Kate reached into the tote bag, took out the three containers of bug spray, tore off the labels, and then put them back in the bag. She took the labels to the kitchen sink, struck a match, and burned them. She walked back to the living room, picked up the bags, walked to the bedroom, and placed the bags on a side chair.

"Time to get in shape," she said; then, she walked the length of the house ten times. Afterward, she seated herself in the recliner to take a break. It was six o'clock.

At five after six, the front door opened, and Sara walked into the foyer. "It's me, honey, I'm home!" she said loudly.

Kate got up from the recliner and walked quickly to meet her mother. "Mother, I'm happy to see you. It's been a long day. How was your day?"

"Do you know I enjoy being at the café? Like we've said many times, some of the people are obnoxious, but most are pleasant. Some have great stories, and some just tell you everything that's happening in their lives. Hey, have you had dinner?"

"No, I waited for you. I wouldn't have dinner when I know my mother's coming home."

"What a sweet daughter you are! I just happened to bring dinner for two. I have special connections at a café, you know."

"Do tell."

They laughed.

"What's the fare tonight?"

"Well, let's see what I have in my little bag. Ah! What about a salad, baked salmon, and a baked sweet potato…all fresh?"

"Yum, yum. Sounds delicious."

"If you'll go to the table, I'll have it spread out by the time you get there."

"Do you want tea? I have a pitcher someone made for me."

"I will have tea with several cubes of ice, please."

Kate poured tea, then they sat down and began eating.

"Mother, I've been thinking…"

"Oh, no!"

"Yes, Mother. Why don't we go to see Christmas Town at Disneyworld in December? Do you remember the street with millions of lights?"

"I do. You were only thirteen. We had such a good time, didn't we? And yes, I'd love to go. We could stay in one of the Disney properties and have a great time."

"Great! We haven't been on a trip in such a long time. Now, I'm excited!"

Sara laughed. "Now, you sound like you did when you were thirteen."

Kate giggled.

"Mother, I'm going out for an hour or so tomorrow night, so I'll be late for dinner."

"Anything I can help you with?" Sara said.

"No, it's sorta personal, something only I can do."

Sara looked at Kate's eyes and was silent for a moment then said, "I have a lotta faith in you. I've taught you well, and you've been an excellent student. Just use caution and the utmost care in everything you do. You're the love in my life, and I wouldn't want anything to happen to you."

"Mother, I promise I'll use the utmost care in everything I do."

Sara smiled. "Wanna watch TV?"

"I do."

They finished eating, cleaned the table, and moved to the den. Sara excused herself at nine o'clock to get ready for bed.

"Sleep tight, Mother."

"Good night, honey."

Kate stood up and then bent down and touched her toes. She repeated the same exercise fourteen times; then, she extended her arms above her head and lowered them to her sides fifteen times. She then repeated both exercises. After that, she read a novel about the trials and tribulations a young woman faced after her husband was killed in Afghanistan. Later, she fell asleep.

At five-thirty in the morning, she felt her mother kiss her on the forehead. She opened her eyes to speak, but her mother had already walked to the door and was on the way out.

"I love you," Kate said, and then went back to sleep.

She woke up at seven o'clock. "The day of the night is upon us," she said. She had toast and coffee and watched TV as she ate. Everyone was talking about parties for Halloween. She reminded herself to get candy for the trick or treaters.

At eight o'clock, the phone rang. Kate looked at the display and saw that it was Ken. "Good morning," she said.

"Good morning! How are you?"

"I'm fine, and yes, we're still on for tonight at six-thirty at your place."

Ken laughed. "You know me too well," he said.

"We'll catch up on everything tonight," Kate said.

"I can't wait."

"See you tonight. Goodbye," Kate said. She clicked off her phone and then walked the length of the house for fifteen times. After that, she did twenty squats. When she finished, she went to the bathroom and looked at herself in the mirror. "My God!" she said. "I look like I've been hit by a truck. I have to cover the yellow under my eye for sure, and the charcoal on my cheek has to go too."

For the next three hours, Kate applied makeup, took it off because she wasn't satisfied, and then reapplied it…four different times. Finally, she looked at herself, turned her head from side to side, and nodded.

It was twelve o'clock. Kate had a sandwich that Sara had made and left in the refrigerator, and then walked the length of the house ten times. After napping in the recliner until three-thirty, she went to her closet and decided on what outfit to wear for the evening. She chose a tan pair of knee-length shorts, a light green silk blouse, and a medium-length darker green scarf, which she wore around her neck tied in a loose knot. She chose a pair of sandals with two-inch heels.

At ten minutes to six, she walked to her bedroom, got the tote bag, and then carefully dumped its contents onto her bed. She picked up each piece, marked it off in her mental inventory, and placed it carefully in the bag. When she finished, she picked up the bag, walked out of the house and down the steps. She walked around to the passenger side of the car, opened the door and placed the bag on the passenger seat, and then walked around the car, got in, and began driving. "Time for some kinky sex," she said.

At twenty minutes after six, she drove into Ken's driveway. The year had rolled into deep fall, and the sizzling summer days were forgotten. The leaves had been drifting from their mother trees for a month now, and the weather had turned chilly. The night noises hadn't changed though. The air was filled with a continuous buzz of sounds from tree frogs, crickets, and night prowlers. They still made the same noises they made at the height of summer.

Kate turned off the car, collected the tote bag, and walked to Ken's front door. She rang the doorbell, and Ken opened it immediately.

"You're early! My god, you look great!" Ken said and reached out to hold her.

"Huh-uh. Kinky sex first," Kate said, holding the tote bag close to her body.

Ken looked at her for a moment, and then a broad smile burst across his face. "You have my attention…big time!"

"Good. Let's go to your bedroom."

Ken's eyes lit up like a thousand candles; then, he did a military about-face and led her toward his bedroom. His house was a ranch-style structure, built in the seventies, and the living quarters were all on one level consisting of sixteen hundred square feet. Although it was an older house, he had furnished it with modern furniture. A lot of straight wood furniture with some metal pieces were placed strategically in every room except the kitchen.

"Let's hop in bed," Ken said.

"No, no, leave your clothes on. Now, we need that straight-back wooden chair that's in the den," Kate said; then she lowered the tote bag to the floor close to the bed.

"Got it!" Ken said, and then rushed out of the bedroom. He returned with the chair, grinning. "What's next?"

"The fifty-pound weights that go on your barbells…we need eight of them."

"In here?" Ken said.

"In here," Kate said.

Ken rushed out, then returned in a moment with a fifty-pound weight in each hand.

"Put one here and the other one here," Kate said, pointing to spots two feet apart and close to the three-foot-tall decorative footboard.

"There are only six," Ken said.

"Well, bring the other four plus two forty-five-pound ones."

"This must be really kinky," Ken said, smiling, then rushed out of the bedroom.

Kate lifted the wooden chair and placed it so that the two back legs fitted into the center holes of the weights. The chair was six-inches from the wooden footboard of the bed, so she lifted the chair away from the weights and scooted the weights another twelve inches away from the footboard. From the tote bag, she selected two of the nylon ropes, bent down, and lifted one of the fifty-pound weights. She slipped one end of the rope under the weight and pulled it out through the hole in the middle of the weight. She carefully pulled the end with the slipknot to the front leg of the chair, then repeated the same steps with the other rope.

She stood up, and then lifted the chair and placed it back over the weights with the two back legs in the holes of the weights.

"I'm back!" Ken said, his voice sounding cheerful and his smile as big as ever.

"Good! I'm going to tilt the chair back; then you put the weights down so that the front legs go in the holes of the weights."

"Alright! I love the suspense! I just can't wait!"

"More weights," Kate said.

Ken rushed off and brought two more fifty-pound weights, and then rushed out again and returned with two forty-five-pound weights. Kate lifted the chair and instructed Ken to stack one weight on top of each weight that had been placed on the carpet. When he finished, each corner had a stack of two weights. Next, Kate lifted the chair and placed it so that each leg of the chair was inserted in the holes of the weights.

"Well, now what?" Ken said, his voice impatient.

"It's almost show time," Kate said. "You're going to sit in the chair, and I'm going to secure you so you can't move."

"How's that gonna work if I can't move?"

"I'm doing the moving. You're going to squirm out of your mind, but it'll be like you've never experienced."

Ken slapped his hands. "Let's get at it!" he said, then backed up to the chair and sat down.

Kate reached to the bed and pulled off the top sheet and looked at the label. It read: "100% cotton." She smiled.

"Okay, let's get you naked," she said, and then pulled him from the chair, unbuttoned his pants, and let them fall to the floor.

"Your shorts and shirt are next." She pulled them off and let them drop. "Okay, let's cover you," she said, and then spread the sheet over Ken leaving only his head exposed.

"This is getting dramatic."

Kate bent down at the front of the chair, grabbed the end of the rope with the slipknot, then said, "Hold your foot up. I'm going to slip this over it."

"Alright, but I'm telling you, the suspense keeps growing."

"Okay, good. Now, let's do the other one," Kate said, and then slipped the rope around Ken's foot. She scooted to the back of the chair and with a lot of effort pulled the other end so that the rope was taut; then she tied it off. She repeated the same technique with the other rope.

"Time for the hands," she said and pulled the handcuffs out of the tote.

"We're doing what?" Ken said, his voice high-pitched.

"I told you this is special. You can't move. I'm doing all the moving. Now, drop your hands and put them behind the chair."

Ken obliged, and Kate slipped the handcuffs around his wrists and locked them.

"One more little piece," Kate said, and then she reached into the bag, pulled out the third rope, slipped the slipknot around his neck, and tied the other end to the back of the chair.

"You're beginning to scare me."

"The good part's about to happen," she said, and then reached into the bag, got one of the spray bottles of flea and tick spray, and sprayed the bed and the footboard.

"What's that smell?" Ken said.

"It's to make you hot, darling," Kate said, and then pulled out another bottle and sprayed the back of the chair with a trail of spray leading to the bedroom curtains. She emptied the bottle on the curtains.

"Just one more finishing touch, sweetheart," she said, and then pulled out the third bottle and sprayed on Ken's hair. Then, she walked to the front of the chair and emptied the bottle on the sheet that covered Ken.

"Hey, what're you doing?" Ken yelled.

"One more item, darling," Kate said, and then placed the three empty bottles in the tote bag and pulled out the fireplace lighter. She stood back as far as her reach would allow then flicked the lighter. Suddenly, the fumes from the spray ignited in a blue hue. Kate jumped back. Before her backward motion stopped, the entire space burst into flames with intense heat. The heat engulfed her and prevented her from breathing. Her face felt as if the flames were enveloping her. Her eyes stung, and her vision was impaired. Panicking, she backed up awkwardly and hastily into the next room. Still feeling threatened, she backed up until she slammed against the opposite wall of the room.

Through the flames, Ken screamed, then screamed again and again and again. The screams were repetitive at first, but soon they became a long continuous, high-pitched sound. Noises came from Ken's chair… an eerie banging against the floor. Even though the weights prevented movement from the chair, it still banged and banged and banged.

Less than a minute passed before Ken's screams drifted into a low roar. His sound was barely audible over the roaring of the flames, which now consumed all the room. A shrill cry sounded, and then there was nothing but an uncontrolled, raging fire.

"You'll never hit me again," Kate said, her voice sounding deep and low as if she were in a tunnel. Her face and eyes continued to burn. She realized she should leave immediately, so she walked out of the house holding the tote bag, got in her car, and drove toward her home. On the way, she pulled in behind a K-Mart store and threw the three empty cans of bug spray into their dumpster. Then she drove home.

CHAPTER 12

The morning rush was over. Kate breathed deeply. She had spent the entire weekend applying oil and lotion to her face, ears, and arms. An inspection of her face, on late afternoon Sunday, using her bathroom mirror did not reveal any burns or redness to her face or arms. She had walked onto the deck at the back of her house and inspected her face in the natural light, but did not see any evidence that her face had been burned or discolored in any way. She had gone back into the house relieved that she looked her natural self.

Monday mornings were interesting because everyone was telling about their exploits over the prior weekend. Most people were getting their yards and gardens ready for winter. One customer related how he had raked leaves into a big pile and backed his pickup truck close to the pile. He and his two sons took turns jumping into the pile of leaves from his truck bed.

The café door opened, and Kate's thoughts were interrupted. A man dressed in a suit and tie walked into the café. He was six feet tall with dark wavy hair, and his face was tanned with wrinkles on his forehead.

Deep wrinkles lined the outer corners of his eyes. The way he wore his suit, one could tell he was not a businessman, but a man who wore a suit like a uniform and was active in it all day.

The man walked straight to Kate, and said, "I'm looking for Kate Simmons. Is she here today?"

"I'm Kate, and I'm here today."

The man laughed slightly as if he were embarrassed for not knowing Kate. "Kate…uh, Ms. Simmons, I'm Maurice Walker, a detective with the NPD." The man then flipped open a leather wallet that showed a badge. "You know Ken Cannon, don't you?"

"Yes, we date."

"Are you aware that his house burned Saturday night…with him in it?"

"His house burned with him in it?" Kate asked, her voice high-pitched and with each word enunciated so that each one produced a shock.

"Yes, ma'am…with him in it."

"Is he dead?" Kate asked, her voice again evoking shock.

"He's dead. With you being close and such, I hate to ask what you were doing between six and ten Saturday night."

"Home nursing my rib cage. I had an accident."

"Alone?"

"No, my mother came by about eight, but she stayed only a few minutes."

"Did the accident also hurt your eye?"

"It did."

"When did you last see Ken?"

Kate hesitated for a moment. Walker was definitely attempting to pin her down. She decided to answer with as much truth as possible. "It's been a few days. We had been dating so much that our personal lives had been set aside, so we mutually decided to take a temporary break and catch up with our personal lives." As she spoke, Kate anticipated the next question, and even as she was speaking, she was working on an answer.

"Was Ken ever abusive to you? Mentally or physically?"

"Would you like some coffee?"

The detective looked at her for a moment and then smiled. "Well, yes, I believe I would…just black."

"I'll be in just a minute," Kate said and then walked toward the coffee bar. She thought about the man's questions and suddenly realized that the trail had been created by her hospital stay, her physical appearance, and the lack of a good alibi. She bit her lip as she realized her stupidity. She poured the coffee and took it to the detective.

"You got a nice place here," the detective said.

Kate was shocked at the remark. What happened to the question before she got coffee? Her thoughts raced. She decided to use the break to elaborate and possibly cause the detective to lose his train of thought. "Well, thank you, Detective. Actually, my mother opened the café many years ago. I grew up here in the café. It was really my home; we stayed here so much. Sundays, when we weren't open, my mother and I spent most of the day here. She cleaned while I swept and vacuumed. She was the owner, cook, janitor, and bookkeeper. Running a café isn't fun. You have to love it."

"Well, this is really good coffee, so you learned how to make coffee. I can vouch for that."

"Thank you. I have a great apple pie I whipped up yesterday on my day off. Would you like a piece?"

"A piece of apple pie? How can I pass up a piece of apple pie? My mother wouldn't think much of me if I passed up apple pie. On top of that, I missed breakfast this morning."

"Great! I'll be right back," Kate said. She felt her meeting with the detective had changed for the better, which changed her mental state. She felt her confidence returning.

She hurried to the kitchen, cut a piece of pie, and walked confidently back to the detective.

"Well, let's try this," he said, then took a large bite. His eyes grew large, and he smiled. "This," he said, pointing to the pie, "is the greatest! This is the best apple pie I've ever tasted. Is this from your mother?"

"Actually, it started with her recipe, but I added a couple of ingredients, and viola. Sara/Kate's apple pie!"

"You got a winner! I mean, you got a winner for sure! Listen, I've used too much of your time. If you have a paper plate, I'll take this with me."

"Oh, sure." Kate got a paper plate and wrapped up the pie for him in aluminum foil.

"I'll be in touch," the detective said, and took the pie and left.

The meeting left Kate with a lot of questions. Had she convinced the detective? Would he snoop around and be back? Did Ken have a lot of good friends, which would take a long time to interview? Would Detective Walker get bogged down and let the case get cold?

She decided to call her mom. She used the pay phone in the hallway near the restrooms because, although the telephone company had discontinued service, the telephone still worked and calls were not traceable due to the lack of official service.

"Hello."

"Mom, I just have a second. Is it okay if I drop in to see you tonight?"

"Sure, honey. Around eightish?"

"Yes, I'll see you then."

"Goodbye, sweetie."

Kate delved into the chores at the café to kill time. It was difficult working and talking to customers when the meeting with the detective weighed on her mind.

Finally, the end of the day came and she drove to her mother's house. She walked to the front door and knocked.

The door opened and her mother greeted her with a hug.

"Mother, there's something very serious I need to discuss with you."

"Well, honey, let's walk through the house and out to the fire pit. Don't say anything until we get there and look down at the fire pit and talk. I'll turn the porch light on."

They walked through the house, out the back door, and to the fire pit in the backyard.

"These fall nights are turning into winter nights," Sara said, "but the bug noise is eternal. Sounds like a buzz saw."

"Mother…"

"One can never be too careful, dear."

"That's just it, Mother. I failed that test."

"Tell me what's happened."

"Ken…"

"I saw on TV there was a fire in his home and he perished."

"You saw right."

"And you?"

"It was me."

"Well, honey, I completely understand. I can understand the rage in your body, in your soul, and the burning desire to quench it."

"I was dumb, wasn't I?"

"It wasn't the smartest thing you've ever done, but I still understand."

A detective came by the café today and asked me where I was when the fire started."

"And you said?"

"I told him home, and that you came by about eight, but you only stayed a few minutes. He asked some other questions, but I think he's okay."

"We can never be too sure."

"I guess burning desire played a part," Kate said, emphasizing the word "burning".

They both laughed.

"You have to remember, my dear, there are many products that mimic a heart attack, and some are just not traceable."

"I know, Mother."

"But the present is here. We need to find a great female attorney, one that's smart, feisty, and hates men."

"Do you mind doing the research?"

"Of course not, but I'll go to the library to do research and make my calls. You can never be too careful."

"Thank you for being my mother."

"The pleasure's all mine. Let's go inside, have some coffee, and talk about the weather."

Kate smiled and hugged her mother.

They went inside, had coffee, and discussed recipes for the café. At nine o'clock, Kate said, "Mother, I have to go home and get some rest."

"You're welcome to stay here."

"I know you would just love it if I stayed, but I need to go home and do all the things that a person living alone does."

Sara smiled. "Well, be careful and keep me informed of all the things happening at the café."

"I will, Mother. Good night."

Back home, Kate wrote in her journal before turning in.

Dear Journal,

November 5, 2010

Today, I walked carefully along the crest of a great mountain and watched both sides of the path. I worried that I might get too close and lose my balance, which would certainly cause me to topple into a gorge. With the help of my heritage and my strong disposition, I shall avoid any disaster that hides along the path waiting for a weak moment. Nay, it shall not happen.

I will write again soon.

Ken's funeral was the next Wednesday, but Kate didn't attend.

For the next day and the following three days, she got up early, went to the café, and worked as if she were training for a great marathon. On Saturday, just as she was getting ready to close, Detective Walker strolled into the café. Kate looked at him and felt a twang in her stomach. She reminded herself that she must act as if he came to the café every day...act natural, chitchat. "Well, you're out late, Detective," she said.

"Do you have any of that great coffee left?" he said.

"I do. You take it black if I remember correctly," Kate said, and started walking to the kitchen.

"Good memory," he said.

She looked back and smiled, "Got to in this business."

She got the coffee pot, poured a cup, and set it down in front of him.

"Thank you, and again, you have a great memory."

"And again, I'm in the restaurant business. A good memory's one of the requirements."

"I never thought of it that way, but you're right. I've seen food service people take food orders and just stand there with no pen, no paper, no nothing."

"It's a gift. It takes a lot of mental training to be able to take multiple orders, return to the kitchen or computer to turn it in, get interrupted by other customers on the way, and still remember what orders you just took. What brings you out this way, Detective? It's Saturday. No weekend plans?"

The detective laughed. "You know, you're right though. You hit the nail right on the head. I was in the neighborhood, and I said, 'Maurice, why don't you stop in at Kate's place and have some coffee?'" He looked at Kate and smiled, then took a gulp of coffee.

"Do you work Sundays strolling around neighborhoods?"

"No, I'm going to lay low. I have this huge boxer, and I'm going to take him outside and just scrub him good. It'll be winter soon, so we're going to beat the cold. Do you have any pets?"

Kate thought about the question for a moment, then took an inventory in her head about Ken and about friends who had pets. Failing to think of anything that might prove to be a threat or a revelation about her past or present security, she said, "No, I don't, Detective. That's one of the disadvantages of being in the restaurant business. You just don't have time for a lot of things other people enjoy."

"Well, that's a shame. You're exactly like me. Work just takes too much darn time," he said. He took the last sip of coffee. "Well, I'm getting outta here so you can go home. It's getting a little chilly. I hope you have a jacket."

"I do. Thank you. Have a nice Sunday with your boxer, Detective."

"I will. Good night."

Thoughts rolled rapidly through Kate's head after Walker left. Why would he just drop in? Why did he ask if I had pets? Does he know something, and he's just playing with me? Has he found something and he's fishing for more?

She decided to call her mother; so she again called Sara from the pay phone. "Mom, do you mind if I drop by for a few minutes?"

"Of course not, darling. Do you want a bowl of my famous soup?"

"I would like that. I'll see you in about twenty minutes."

"Twenty minutes is fine. I'll see you then," Sara said.

Kate looked around to see if she should do anything before closing. Seeing nothing, she locked up, got in her car, and drove to her mother's house. She felt good being there; maybe because she felt secure; maybe it was because her mother was on her side, regardless she felt free talking with her mother.

"Get in this house, my daughter," Sara said from the doorway.

Kate looked at her mother and rushed up the sidewalk to meet her mother.

"Honey, were you daydreaming?"

Kate laughed. "No, I was just thinking that I enjoy being here. Even though it's fall, your flower beds look fresh, your grass is green, and your trees without leaves look like soldiers-at-attention guarding the place."

"Well, what a romantic you are."

"I take after you, my mother."

Sara reached out and kissed Kate on the forehead. "Get in here. Soup's ready."

Kate followed her mother inside. "Mom, the detective came by tonight. He asked me if…"

"Hold it, honey," Sara said. Then she motioned Kate to follow her outside onto the lawn. Once outside, she motioned again and pointed to a spot fifty feet from the house. When they got there, Sara looked at the ground and said, "Hold your head down when you talk, honey. Okay, you were saying?"

"The detective came by. He asked me if I had animals."

"Why would he ask that?"

"If I used my wild imagination, I would say that he or someone has discovered that I bought some bottles of flea and tick spray."

"And you used it?"

"I did."

"Lucky for you I've found a great attorney. She's a westerner. She's been the defender in forty-three felony cases. She's forty-three and zero, never lost a case, but she's like a woman you'd meet on the street—down to earth."

"You've done well. You get a promotion. What's her name?"

"Amy Pratt."

"When do we meet her?"

"She can come here at nine tomorrow morning if you're available. I have to call her tonight to confirm. She's in town for a meeting…lucky for you."

"Let's do it," Kate said.

"Why don't you spend the night here with me?"

"Do you have an extra toothbrush?"

"Do I have an extra toothbrush? Of course, I have an extra toothbrush. I have three extra toothbrushes."

"Great! You have yourself a tenant."

Sara smiled. "Let's have some soup and when we get inside, we'll chitchat about everything women chitchat about, but we'll not have one word spoken about what we've been talking about. Got it?"

"Got it. Sounds good. Besides, it's getting chilly out here."

They went inside, and Sara called Amy. She talked for a moment, and then clicked off the phone. "It's all set for nine in the morning.

This is a get-acquainted meeting, nothing else."

"Perfect! Thank you."

They ate, talked about how both of them had lived at the restaurant for nearly twenty years, then turned in for the night.

The next morning, Sara opened the door to Kate's room and said in a low voice, "Honey, wake up."

Kate moaned and said with a sleepy voice, "What time is it?"

"It's a quarter of seven. Do you want to get a quick shower and have an egg and toast at seven-thirty?"

"Mother, that's only forty-five minutes from now," Kate said in a whinny voice.

Sara walked to her bed and kissed her on the forehead. "What a beautiful daughter I have! Now, get up and get going." She spoke in a soft tone a mother would use for a small child. "Now, peek outside. It's a five-star day...sun's shining, it's cool, humidity's low, and the wind just plays with the tips of your hair."

"Okay! Okay, I'm up, and I'll peek outside. Will the wind comb my hair?"

"Silly," Sara said, and then left the room, made coffee and breakfast.

At a quarter after seven, she went back to Kate's bedroom door and said, "Will you be ready in fifteen minutes?"

"Yes, Mother, and I peeked outside."

"Good girl!"

After breakfast, they cleared the table of everything except their coffee cups, and at nine o'clock sharp, the doorbell rang. Sara, who was closely followed by Kate, walked to the door and opened it.

"Amy Pratt?" Sara said.

"At your service," Amy said, smiling. "And you would be Sara, and you would be Kate."

Amy's voice was clear and direct. It had the same enthusiasm and confidence of a used car salesperson.

"Correct on all counts," Sara said.

Kate looked at Amy and made mental notes about her physical

appearance. She was taller than the average woman. Kate judged her to be about five foot nine. She wore a gray business suit with a white blouse and a simple white gold necklace. She was trim, and Kate thought she was elegant with her shoulder-length dark hair and dark eyes.

"Kate, I must compliment you, and all I'm doing is stating a fact; you are a stunningly beautiful woman."

"Thank you, and you likewise," Kate said.

Amy laughed. "I wish all the judges thought that."

"We saved a coffee for you if you indulge," Sara said.

"That would be delightful," Amy said, drawing out the word "delightful."

"Why don't you two have a seat in the living room, and I'll bring coffee," Sara said.

"After you," Amy said, nodding at Kate.

Kate walked into the living room followed by Amy; they sat in chairs opposite each other.

"Kate, I just love to come to this part of the country and at this time of year. With rolling hills up to the edge of the mountains and those beautiful trees turning all shades of yellow, brown, and red…well, it would just make the most wonderful painting. I would love to go to the mountains and breathe in the fresh, mountain air. Wouldn't that be delightful?" Amy said, her voice sounding as if she were auditioning for a part in a play.

"I love them as well, and it would be delightful just to gaze at the beauty that Mother Nature has given us," Kate said.

"Well, back to the business at hand. Sara has filled me in about what's going on in your life. I have snooped around the police department and know they haven't finished their investigation of Ken's death. Until they finish and until you become a person of interest, there's no reason for us to discuss anything. So, if it's okay with you, we'll just visit tonight. However, if anything different happens, here's my card. You call me immediately!" Amy said, her voice now direct, precise, and her words pronounced perfectly.

Kate took the card and said, "That I will do. Thank you."

For the next hour, the three women talked and drank coffee, and then Amy left.

"What do you think?" Sara said.

"I can understand why she's never lost a case. No one can get a word in edgewise, but I'm happy that she's a friend. I'm happy that she's around…you know what I mean?"

"Believe it or not, I believe I do," Sara said.

"Mother, I need to make up my bed and go home."

"Honey, while you do that, I'll be making a sandwich for us. And we can have some leftover soup if you'd like."

"Deal on the sandwich and deal on the soup. I'll be done in thirty minutes."

Kate went to her bedroom, and Sara went to the kitchen. Later, they had soup and a sandwich. Then Kate left Sara's home. As she walked to her car, falling leaves gently brushed her face. She smiled, and bent down and picked up a red leaf speckled with yellow. It had three points and had enough growth and life left that kept it intact. She used its stem and spun it slowly looking at each side as it turned. "I'm taking you to reside beside my journal," she said. Then she got in her car and drove home.

Once inside, she walked to her desk and placed the red leaf beside her journal. "Rest well, my beauty," she said.

She did some laundry and watched TV, but she felt uneasy. She walked to her desk and pulled out her journal, opened it, and began writing.

November 14, 2010

Dear Journal,

Have you ever found yourself just wandering around with no objective that you could name? Have you ever felt uneasy and didn't know why? Have you ever walked down a street in the dark with no clue as to where you're going? I'm experiencing all those things. I feel as if I've fallen from the mountain, landed in the valley, and have no means to extract myself.

For lack of thoughts, I'll sign off.

Kate put her journal in the desk, got a sheet of paper from her printer, and wrote "What I Own and What I Owe" as a caption. She began itemizing the items she owned, and she became keenly interested in being precise. After much thought and review of old bills of sales and invoices, she finished the list of what she owned. She then started the list of what she owed. She made columns of who she owed, the monthly payment, and the date the different debts would be paid off. She then went through her bills and recorded the information. When she finished, she printed three copies, one she placed inside the bound journal, the second copy on top of her desk. She would put it in her lock box at the bank. She would give her mother a copy as well.

Feeling restless, she walked the length of the house looking out the windows. She felt trapped, as if the walls were closing in on her, so she decided to take her mother's copy of the "Own and Owed" letter to her. She left her house, got in her car, and drove to her mother's house.

Her mother looked startled to see her. "What's wrong, honey?"

"I'm sorry if I startled you, Mother. I just caught up on my bookkeeping and wanted you to have a copy of it."

"An asset list?" Sara said.

"And an owed list."

Sara frowned. "Are you okay, honey?"

"I'm fine, Mother. This is just something I thought of doing and wanted you to have a copy since you are not only my mother but my best friend."

"How darling," Sara said and hugged her. "Do you want anything to eat or drink?"

"No, Mother, thank you. I'm going back home and do some cleaning."

"You can stay if you want, you know."

"I know, but I need to catch up with some things. You know how little time the restaurant people have."

"Many years, my daughter."

"Good night, Mother."

***

Kate drove home, picked up a newspaper from her sidewalk, and went inside her home. She had an egg and tomato sandwich on toast, walked slowly to the bathroom, and stared at herself in the mirror. "Mirror, mirror, on the wall…" she said, her words trailing off to a low, indistinguishable sound. She brushed her teeth, showered, took a PM capsule, and went to bed.

She awakened at five the next morning, got ready for work, and then drove to the café and began her daily routine.

The workweek passed without incidence except Kate began a special breakfast promotion at the café—pancakes, all you can eat, and hot chocolate for five dollars. Pancakes came in every variety under the sun…apple, blueberry, strawberry, cherry, chocolate, pecan, banana, and many more. The promotion was such a hit that Kate called her mother and asked why they hadn't run the promotion in the past.

One patron said, "Kate, I scraped frost off my windshield this morning and when I got here at seven, you had that hot chocolate waiting for me. I'm telling you, it's the best I've ever had. I hope you keep on offering it."

"You can bet on it," Kate said.

Saturday came and Kate was looking forward to having Sunday off. The promotion had kept the kitchen crew busy, and Kate had done double duty, working the kitchen and the dining room hardly stopping to eat herself.

As the clock rolled to seven, she prepared to close, but the door opened, and a familiar figure strolled into the dining room.

"Detective Walker! You're out late again!"

"Well, so I am. I was just driving by here, and I said to myself, 'Self, why don't you stop by and see Kate Patterson?' As you might suspect, I got no response, so I stopped anyway. Am I going to put you out?"

"Absolutely not! I kept the coffee hot for you. You stop by here every Saturday. Remember?"

"Well, that I do, and I'd welcome that coffee."

"I'll be right back," Kate said. Then she walked to the kitchen, poured a cup of coffee, and walked back to Detective Walker. "Black, the way you like it, sir."

"Well, thank you, ma'am," Detective Walker said, and then sipped the coffee. "You know, I've been thinking about my ol' boxer and that I was going home and just scrub the fire outta him."

"I do remember that."

"Well, then, do you remember my asking you if you had any pets, and you said you didn't?" the detective said, and then took another large sip of coffee.

"I remember that too. You seem to have pets on your mind today."

The detective's face moved as if he were about to laugh, but he didn't. "I do think about pets a lot. I don't know why, but I do. Take you, for instance. Why would a woman like you who don't have any pets go to a store and buy flea and tick spray? Oh, and we know it was you 'cause we got you on camera just as clear as day."

Kate remained silent while she processed the detective's statement.

"You don't have to answer that," the detective said. "You know, it's the oddest thing. You know your friend, Ken…Ken Cannon? He was set afire with that stuff. Our lab, now they are sure of something. They can come up with some of the craziest things, can break a case wide open. And something more, do you know Ken was handcuffed? Our lab discovered that too. Now, don't ask me how they did that with most of the bones disintegrated. And the metal! Surely, you'd think it would melt to nothing. But, no, the lab said that Ken's hands were handcuffed behind him, and he was just burned to a crisp. Whadda you say about that?"

Kate was silent for a moment, and then said in a low voice, "I don't know what to say."

"Well, of course, you don't. There's something else we have on camera," the detective said. He looked at Kate for a long moment and said, "You buying handcuffs. The funny thing about these cameras. They're all over the place. Ms. Patterson, I've been studying you this week. I know you were at the hospital. I know you were there because someone let it out on you, and I'd be willing to bet that person was Ken Cannon. Before I do anything official, I want you to call your mother, Sara. I've known her for years and years. I want you to tell her that you're going to have to go downtown with me, and you're gonna be there for a few days; that is, until a judge sets bail, and if you make bail, well, you'll be out on the street again."

Kate stood erect and stared at the detective until both of them felt uncomfortable. "Are you arresting me, Detective Walker?"

"Yes, ma'am, I am. There are two officers just outside the front door, and they're gonna take you downtown where you'll be charged for the murder of Ken Cannon. Now, call your mother and quick. We're runnin' out of time."

Kate turned away from the detective.

"You're goin' for your phone?"

"Yes."

"I'll go with you…just in case."

Kate walked to the kitchen, her profile stiff at first, but her movement became smooth and fluid after her first six steps. "Do you want to listen?" she asked the detective as she picked up the phone.

"I'll just wait over by the counter."

Kate dialed her mother's number. "Mother, I have Detective Walker here at the café…"

"You do?" her mother said, her voice high-pitched.

"Yes, he's come to arrest me for the murder of Ken Cannon."

"Is he taking you away?"

"Yes, I'll be in the downtown jail until the judge sets bail. Meanwhile, will you call Amy and tell her I'm downtown and would like to see her. Will you keep the café going?"

"Of course, darling. I'll do both those things. Is there anything I can do for you right now?"

"Yes, get my journal out of my desk and take it to your house," Kate said, trying to whisper but talking loud enough for her mother to hear her.

"I will do all those things."

"Thank you, Mother. See you later."

CHAPTER 13

Kate stayed in a cell at the county jail Saturday night and all day Sunday. On Monday, after a breakfast of watery scrambled eggs, soggy bacon, a hard biscuit, and watered-down orange juice, Amy Pratt visited her in her cell.

"How're you doing?" Amy said.

"Well, I didn't walk my usual three miles yet, so I'm really upset."

Amy's facial features changed to a smile. "We'll see what we can do about that, but first, I came just to talk a little bit about how we're going to proceed with your case. You know, of course, what you're charged with. How do you feel about that?"

"Do you mean if I'm guilty of not?"

"That's more direct than I was thinking, but since we're there, I have to know the truth. When we get in the courtroom, I sure as hell don't want any surprises. Are you willing to proceed on those terms?"

"I am. I'll tell you the truth about everything. I'm not in the habit of lying, and I expect the same standard from other people. I'll tell you about Ken Cannon. I'll tell you anything that will help us."

"What about Ken?"

"I tied him up and burned his ass."

"Why?"

"He beat the literal hell out of me. He cracked two or three of my ribs, almost put out an eye, and nearly broke my jaw."

"Why did he beat you?"

"From the very first day we dated, he bought tickets to every concert, every play, every sporting event, and we ate at the top restaurants. He took me to shows and plays in New York, St. Louis, Atlanta, and more places than I can remember offhand. I questioned where he was getting the money, but he never said anything. I thought he was a successful man, and he knew his business. But then my mother overheard that he had taken a second mortgage on his home and that he was behind with both mortgages to the extent that he was about to lose his home. So, I just casually presented the question to him, and he went into a rage.

"He hit me in the face with his fist—I'm not sure how many times— and then slung me across the room. I struck the wall so violently that it cracked my ribs. I was semiconscious. Even though he could see my condition, he grabbed me by my hair and struck me again. He yelled at me to never stick my ass in his business again."

"My God! Have you recovered enough so that you can function?"

"I'm a strong person. I'll make it."

"Good. I'll get the hospital records," Amy said. "Had you two ever had an argument before that incident?"

"Never. He seemed to want to please me at every turn, and I was conscious of that."

"The fellow could have been suffering from schizophrenia. I'll check his medical records. The judge will probably have a hearing on Wednesday, and after hearing from both sides, he'll set bail. Do you think your mother can cover the bail?"

"Absolutely. So I'm stuck here until Wednesday at the earliest?"

"You are. I'll see you before Wednesday though. Is there anything I need to tell Sara?"

"I asked her to get my journal from my desk."

"Honey, I'm afraid that didn't work. They had an officer stationed at your home to make sure nothing walked away. I'm sure they have a search warrant to look at every piece of your home. Do you think they'll find anything interesting?"

"Nothing but the journal. Nothing on my computer or anything else."

"Is there anything incriminating in the journal?"

"It's mainly in code that only I know."

"Good. Okay, I'll go. I have a lot of work to do," Amy said, and then called for the guard to let her out, which she did, and left.

Kate looked at her surroundings. There were eight cells in the area, and they were all occupied by women. Some looked dejected, some looked rough in their physical state, and some had facial skin that looked tight and dark as if it had been subjected to the sun and elements and had never received an application of moisturizing lotion. Some were loud and noisy and screamed at the guards. Vulgarity was the going language.

A guard passed and Kate rushed to the front of the cell to speak to her. "Miss…"

The guard turned to look at Kate.

"Miss, is it possible to get some paper and a pen. I want to do some writing."

The guard frowned. "Your name's Kate?"

"Yes, ma'am."

"Kate, you can't have a pen in here. You're being held on a charge of murder, so you can just forget it."

"Thank you," Kate said and for the first time, the seriousness of her situation jolted her. She was in a holding area with criminals; she was considered a criminal herself; she was well out of her peaceful surroundings.

Five minutes passed. She thought about the café, and even though the work was demanding, with no "thank you", it was part of her life. Then she thought about her mother, her best friend. Her mother had given her a career, had tutored her, and was forever present when a problem arose. To keep her mind occupied, she thought about the mountains and how they rose to touch the sky, how they provided a natural nursery for hundreds of trees that competed for sunlight and space, how the entire mass from a distance resembled a gigantic green carpet.

An hour passed. She thought about her relationships with men so far in her life and came to the conclusion that she had not been too successful in her endeavors.

Suddenly, a shrill scream sounded from a cell across from Kate's; a woman grabbed the bars and screamed, "They're comin'! They're comin!" She banged her head on the bars and then screamed again. "Help me! Help me! They got me! They got me!"

Three deputies strolled to the cell and opened it. Two of the deputies struggled with the woman but finally controlled her; the third deputy used a syringe to sedate her. They held her upright. Then a deputy on each side of her supported her and dragged her out of the cellblock.

Kate stood as if she were frozen to the floor. Her eyes fixated on the open space in front of her. Her entire psyche had changed in one second.

"Demons got 'er!" a woman said from an adjoining cell.

Kate didn't move.

"Yo, Red. Ya heard me?"

Kate turned slowly and looked at the woman, a short stocky person with long blond hair that looked like it hadn't been washed in many days. Her arms were short, plump, and puffy-looking. Her face was also plump and puffy-looking, but her light-blue eyes stole the show. They sparkled like fine jewels. Kate asked herself why a woman with such dazzling eyes was now in a jail cell.

"Demons got 'er. Got 'er hook, line, and sinker."

Kate stared at the woman and took a step toward her. Moving as if her shoes were sticking to the floor, Kate moved so that she was three feet from the cell that held the woman. "What do you mean... demons?" she said, her voice faltering slightly.

"I mean demons! Ya gotta feed ``em. If ya don't, they make ya sweat; they make ya feel like somthin' chasin' ya; they make ya jerk; they make ya feel like you're outta your head; they make ya crazee!" the woman said, yelling so that the entire cellblock could hear. She jumped up, grabbed the cell bars, and shouted again, "Crazee! Crazee! Crazee!"

Kate backed up. Obviously, the woman behind the metal bars was just like the one that had been hauled off.

"Demons! Demons! Demons!" the woman yelled, and then sat on the edge of her cot and stared into space.

Kate looked around at the dark world she had suddenly become a part of. When she was part of the "normal" world, she occasionally met an unruly person or a rough person, but she ignored them or went around them and resumed what she'd been doing.

She sat down on the cot, which had a stained mattress with no sheet. She looked at the dirty mattress and asked herself how she had managed to sleep on it for two nights. She must have been in shock those nights, but now her head told her the reality of her existence.

She decided to turn the mattress, so she struggled to lift it only to see that it had urine stains, dirty spots, and general filth. She gagged, and then let it drop back to the frame.

A guard strolled slowly in sight of her cell.

Kate rushed to the bars and said, "Miss, Miss Guard..."

The guard turned slowly and looked at Kate for a long moment. "What now?"

"It's my cot. What do I have to do to get a new one?"

The guard walked slowly so that she was an inch away from the cell bars and so close that Kate felt her breath. "Stay with us another twenty-five years, and we'll get you a new one," the guard said. "Now, find something to occupy your time."

Kate looked at the guard, then took one step back. "Thank you," she said.

The guard smiled and walked away.

"Yo, Red."

Kate turned to the woman in the cell next to her. "Yes."

"Come over here, Red."

Kate thought for a moment and walked closer to the bars that separated her from the woman.

"Say, Red, haf ya ever been to the Big House?"

"The Big House?"

"Yeah, ya know, the Big Pokey. I've been there a coupla times... demons ya know. Got the demons out, an' here I am again."

"You're talking about the penitentiary?"

"Yeah! Yeah, the Big Pokey. Ya been?"

"No, I haven't. What's your name?"

"Name's Cynthia. Red, there's so much ya haf to learn. So much. So much. I guess I haf to teach ya wha' to do. First, they're goin' to shackle ya in a bus. We call it the Black Box. When ya get to the Big House, ya don't talk like we're talkin' now. Ya talk with your hands. Like when ya finish eatin', ya tap on the table. That means ya leavin'. Oh! An' money! Ya don't haf any money in the Big House. Ya haf postage stamps. Yeah, one stamp is a dolla'. If ya want cigarettes, pills, any kind of anything else, ya buy 'em with stamps. That's your money. Got it?"

"You know, I do get it, and I want to thank you for telling me."

"Well, it's no problem at all. Say, do ya see that bitch behind me?"

Kate looked behind Cynthia and then looked throughout the cell, but there was no other person in the cell. So as not to cause a conflict, she said, "I do. Why is she in there with you?"

"She's tryin' to steal my money. She's got the demons. Red, don't ever let the demons near ya. Ya got it?"

"I do, and I'll never let them in. Hey, it's time to eat."

Cynthia looked toward the front of her cell as a paper plate was slipped underneath the bars. "Slop for the piggys! Slop for the piggys!" she chanted.

Kate picked up her plate, which had no fork, spoon, or knife. Only a frankfurter, which had been boiled, a bun, half of an apple, which had not been peeled and still had the core and seeds, and a Styrofoam cup of water composed her lunch.

"I hate apples!" Cynthia shrieked.

Kate walked hurriedly to the bars that separated them. "Cynthia, I'll trade you a hot dog for your apple."

Cynthia looked curiously at her. "You will?"

"I will. I don't want you to eat apples if you don't like them."

"Red, ya got yourself a deal."

"I'll be right back with your hot dog," Kate said, and then stepped over to pick up the hot dog with her fingers. She rushed back to the bars. "Stick the apple through the bars with your right hand, and I'll stick the hot dog through the bars so you can take it with your left hand," Kate directed. Some strange instinct had kicked into her being. She had only been locked up for a weekend, but survival savvy had surfaced.

Cynthia stuck her apple through the bars.

"Cynthia, I can't reach it from there. Stick it through a little farther."

Cynthia did as Kate had asked; Kate took hold of the apple with her left hand and stuck the hot dog through the bars with her right hand.

"I wasn't goin' to keep your apple," Cynthia said, her jaws positioned lower and her lips bulged out slightly.

"Oh, no, no, no! I know you weren't. I just didn't want it to fall on this filthy floor," Kate said. "You're my friend. You're the only friend I have in here."

"I am?"

"Yes, yes, I get to talk with you whenever you feel like talking. We're just like that," Kate said, crossing one finger over the other and holding her hand so Cynthia could see.

"So we're buds?"

"We sure are. Buddies we are, and you can take that to the bank."

Cynthia snickered. "I like you," she said, and then stuck the entire hot dog in her mouth.

Kate retreated to her cot, ate Cynthia's half-apple, ate the bottom part of her hot dog bun, and sat for several minutes. "I must remember all this for my journal," she said in a low, whisper. Then she ate her half-apple, the top part of her hot dog bun, and drank half of her cup of water. She saved the remaining half-cup to rinse her mouth after she cleaned her teeth with hand soap.

"I'm goin' to sleep," Cynthia said in a loud voice.

"Have a good sleep," Kate said, her voice also loud. She sat on the cot with her back and head against the concrete-block wall. She closed her eyes and decided that she would mentally record every day, every encounter with inmates and guards, the lousy food, the filthy cell, and anything else that happened. When she was free again, she would get a leather-bound journal and write down from memory everything she could remember. She thought that she might even write a book and detail all her thoughts, all her experiences, and all her emotions while being locked up. She would have a book cover in black and white with a shadow of a woman, her hands grasping cell bars, and a silhouette of herself looking through the bars. The thoughts lifted her spirits, and she smiled. She lay still and fell asleep.

At four o'clock, her cell door opened, which made a loud, screeching noise, and she awakened.

"Well, sleeping beauty, how are you?" Amy said.

"Hi, Amy. Whoa! I fell asleep. This environment is so restful."

Amy smiled. "We have a lot to cover in a short period of time, so if you don't mind, we'll get with it. I've talked with the district attorney (DA). They have you on camera buying the pet spray; they have you on camera buying the handcuffs plus a witness; they have you on camera getting out of your car at Ken's, going into his house, and then leaving. You got in your car and drove away. Two minutes later, flames sprang from the side of the house."

"How did they get that?"

"Convenience store camera across the street."

"Oh."

"So, if we go into court with a no-guilty plea, we're going to lose, and you can count on a very long sentence. I don't think they would ask for the execution, but even that would not be out of the question."

"What do we do?"

"I've talked to the DA, told him the circumstances, detailed your background, and he's willing to agree to a plea of involuntary manslaughter."

"Where does that put me?"

"It's a Class E felony. Has a sentence of one to six years. The DA is willing for you to describe the attack on your person by Mr. Cannon, which resulted in your severe distress and mental state of mind and caused you to perform an act that you in your normal state of mind could not and would not perform. You were simply unable to reason normally."

Kate looked at Amy, looked at the closet-size cell, then said, "And where would I hang my hat?"

"I have asked the DA if the Tennessee Prison for Women in Nashville would be available."

"I had no idea there was a…a prison in Nashville. Where is it?"

"It's on Stewart's Lane in Northwest Nashville. It has educational and vocational programs; it has a program called Building Entrepreneurships for Success in Tennessee; it has psychological and treatment programs…not that you need those; it has a child visitation program. It's just about a home away from home."

Kate laughed. "Yeah."

"By entering the involuntary plea, we keep a trial out of the newspaper, off TV, and the case will have very little exposure to the outside world. In other words, Sara would run the restaurant, which would be a needed stroke of luck. It's possible you would get on a work program, which would be cool. It's very possible you could do some teaching…

culinary, management, that sort of thing."

"So how much real time do you think I will get?"

"I would think for about one year. After the plea, you'll be confined here...probably for a period of three months."

"You're saying that if I'm lucky, I could be out of this hellhole in a year?"

"With a little luck, good behavior, which I know would exist...yes."

"Amy, this is the most degrading existence anyone can imagine. Even a fiction writer couldn't dream up the degradation that I and all these other people are enduring. The toilet has no paper and none will be issued. That means you must use your finger to clean and then find a way to clean your finger. When the sink would run water, I washed the finger on my left hand twenty times, and then I cleaned my teeth with my fingers on the other hand. Look at this cot. Ten years of filth have settled here. I had a hot dog bun, an apple, and a cup of water for lunch. But, you know, I'm a strong person, and by the grace of god, I will get through this. Tell the DA we'll go with the involuntary manslaughter plea, and let's get this over with."

Amy patted Kate's shoulder. "I admire your strength, and yes, you'll get through this. You'll have to tell the judge at his discretion the circumstances that caused your action. I believe what you told me about Ken's behavior will go a long way to satisfy the judge. The judge, we believe, will be Judge Wilson. He's an advocate for women's rights and supports the Center for Battered Women."

"That's favorable at least."

"And, a medical report on Ken should be in my office as we speak. I have a real hunch that he was seeing a psychiatrist. If that's so, it could be beneficial to our case. And it wouldn't hurt in the least for the court to know that you feared for your life."

"And so shall it be. Do you know anything about women's prisons? Like what are everyday living arrangements like?"

"Well, I know you can buy toilet paper."

"Really?"

"Do you know inmates use postage stamps for money?"

"Cynthia told me," Kate said, pointing to the cell next to hers.

"So, if you have postage stamps, you can buy just about anything…drugs, cigarettes, blankets, soap, food…you name it."

"Sounds like a world within a world," Kate said.

"That it is. There's the guard. My time's up. I'll see you either on Tuesday or Wednesday morning. By the way, you get a shower the morning we go to court."

Kate grabbed her arm. "For real? I get a shower?" she said, her voice high-pitched.

Amy smiled. "Yes, a real shower and maybe a hot shower."

"Oh, my god!"

"Yo, lady, ya a lawyer?"

Any and Kate looked at Cynthia.

"If ya a lawyer, I need one real bad. I can pay ya."

"I'm sorry. My schedule's full," Amy said.

"Will ya pleeze find me a lawyer?"

"I must go. Kate, I'll see you later," Amy said; then a guard opened the cell, and she walked out. She turned to look at Kate as the guard locked the cell, waved and walked away.

Kate walked to the bars separating her from Cynthia. "Cynthia, I'll try to find you a lawyer."

"Will ya…pleeze? I need a lawyer real bad."

"I'll try," Kate said, then walked back to her cot and sat down.

Only a few minutes passed before dinner arrived. It consisted of a piece of bologna between two pieces of bread, six potato chips, and a cup of water. Kate hated bologna, but there wasn't anything to trade with Cynthia. Besides, she was hungry, so she drew an imaginary line down the center of the two pieces of bread; then she mentally cut the bread and bologna into two halves as a sandwich. She decided that one-half of the sandwich would provide her with six bites. There would be only three chips for each half of the sandwich, so she would have to take three bites without a chip for each half of the sandwich.

Having planned her meal, she took a small bite from one-half of the sandwich and chewed slowly. After she convinced herself that it was thoroughly chewed, she swallowed. Next, she carefully picked up the glass of water and sipped slowly but allowed herself only a teaspoon full. She looked forward to the next bite because she would allow herself one chip to eat with it.

For the next forty minutes, she ate slowly and sipped the water until all had been consumed.

CHAPTER 14

"Kate."

Kate jerked from her position on her cot. She had rested in a ninety-degree angle with her back and head against the cement-block wall and her butt and legs on the cot. There was nothing available to put between her legs and the cot, so she had gritted her teeth and made the best of it. She looked toward the bars of her cell and said, "Amy?"

"Good morning, Kate. How are you?"

"Well, I haven't had my morning water yet, but otherwise I'm great."

Amy smiled and looked at her watch. It's two minutes after seven. We're due in court at nine-thirty. It takes twenty minutes to get to court from her. So that means you have a little more than two hours for us to discuss your case, for you to have breakfast, and get a hot shower."

"Get a hot shower?" Kate said, beaming. Her eyes sparkled like polished emeralds.

"I suppose you want the shower first," Amy said, smiling.

"Oh, yes, yes, yes! And my hair...I'll wash my hair!"

"She's getting a shower," Amy said to the guard, who had accompanied her to Kate's cell." She needs a clean jumpsuit, some soap, and some shampoo and conditioner. We're going to the court in two hours, and the judge wants her to look like a human being."

The guard walked away without commenting, then returned in five minutes with all the items Amy had requested. A second guard followed the first.

"And a toothbrush and toothpaste," Amy said to the guard.

"She…" the guard started to say something before Amy cut her off.

"And a hairdryer. We're not sending her to see the judge with wet hair."

Again the guard walked away without any comment.

"Amy, I'm sure happy to have you on my side," Kate said.

"You can't be a sissy when you deal with these people. Of course, when you're on the wrong side of the cell bars, you have to eat their crap. Okay, toothbrush, toothpaste, and hair dryer are here," Amy said. She looked at the guard. "Will you take her to the shower?"

Without speaking, the first guard opened Kate's cell. The second guard standing nearby said, "Follow me."

They walked to the end of the cell block as the inmates in each cell watched their every step; then they took a left turn into a corridor that led to a huge room with cell bars as doors. The guard keyed a code into a keypad mounted on the wall, and a door made of bars opened. A huge tiled area spread out beyond the doors. Ten shower heads protruded from the walls with no barriers. It was simply one gigantic shower stall where ten individuals could shower simultaneously. Three built-out areas were situated opposite the showers, which Kate assumed were stations for guards.

"In here," a guard said, pointing to a four-foot area with walls on both sides. "In here. You're taking a shower in the private space. You're a special guest," the guard said, sneering at Kate. "Here's your soap, your shampoo, and your conditioner. We wouldn't want your hair not be shiny. Your toothbrush and toothpaste are here too. It's all here in this mesh bag."

Kate took the bag, which was small enough to fit into the palm of her hand. It resembled a jewelry bag that closed by pulling strings on two sides, which tightened the top. Kate pulled the bag open to see all the hotel-sized items. She was disappointed because she had imagined getting a large bar of Dove soap with a lotion that she could use and keep and know that it was her very own.

"You got twenty minutes," the guard said.

The sound startled Kate for a moment, but she looked at the guard and said, "Thank you." She took off her jumpsuit and tossed it so that it landed on top of the shower wall.

"She doesn't look tough enough to murder anybody," one guard said to the other.

"Yeah," the second guard said.

Kate looked around the shower. She placed the mesh bag on a small shelf by the faucets and turned on the hot water. She couldn't remember her routine of taking a shower, but she reminded herself she had only twenty minutes, so she stuck her head under the water and felt the warm liquid cascade over her hair and drain down her face. "Oh, my god!" she said in a low voice so the guards couldn't hear.

She removed the tiny bottle of shampoo from the bag and looked at it for a moment, and then poured one-half of it into her palm, rubbed her hands together, and worked it into her hair. It didn't lather well. She felt probably because she hadn't washed her hair in such a long time. She rinsed, then hurriedly applied the second half of shampoo. Sure enough, it lathered nicely. She rinsed and then reached for the conditioner.

"Ten minutes," a guard said in a loud voice.

"Thank you," Kate said, now feeling rushed but thinking what a joy it would be to have all the time she wanted to treat her body to a long, leisurely, soothing shower.

She poured the entire bottle of conditioner into her palm and worked it into her hair while telling herself that she had already used one minute. She thought about her journal and how she wanted to record her thoughts and the sensations she felt when the warm water touched her, then drained down the length of her body immersing her entire being as she stood.

Feeling more pressure, she hurriedly took the tiny bar of soap from the bag, wet it, rubbed it between her hands until it lathered, soaped the top part of her body, and then soaped her lower torso, legs, and feet. Even with the rushed condition, she felt as if her body was saying "thank you" over and over.

"Five minutes," the guard said in a loud, harsh voice.

Silently, Kate quickly made a schedule…one and one-half minutes to rinse her hair, one minute to rinse her body, and two and one-half minutes to dry off and pull on her jumpsuit. She started immediately with her schedule and just as the guard yelled that her time was up, she pulled up her jumpsuit and reached to get the empty items from the shelf.

"Leave all that stuff on the shelf. Your neighbors need a job," the guard said.

Kate looked at the empty boxes that held shampoo, conditioner, and soap and would have been happy to put them in the trash, but she did exactly as the guard ordered.

"Step out here, Miss Privileged Child," the second guard said.

Kate stepped out of the shower, through the doorway in the cell bars, and into the corridor.

The first guard locked the cell and said, "Follow her and pointed to the second guard."

Kate followed the second guard and was flanked by the first guard. The inmates held onto their cell bars and watched them just as they had done when they went to the shower.

"Hey, Red, what'd they did to ya?" one of the inmates yelled.

Both the guards and Kate were silent and looked straight ahead.

"Betcha she got a shower!" another inmate yelled.

Then a chorus of sounds started. "Betcha got a shower! Betcha got a shower! Betcha got a shower!"

Amy stood in the corridor and met them as they arrived. "Let's go inside," she said, pointing to Kate's cell. They walked inside, and Amy whispered, "Feel better?"

Kate smiled. "I do," she said in a low voice.

"Here goes the business part," Amy said. "I got the scoop on Ken. He was not seeing a psychiatrist, but it seems he had a very colorful past. He was in trouble throughout high school; he couldn't tolerate college, so he dropped out; he had differences with his neighbors and was cited twice for disorderly conduct. I wrote a brief that we will present it to the judge. The DA's office is sticking to their guns; they still agree to the terms we discussed earlier."

"One to six?" Kate said.

"Yes. Do you have any thoughts or questions?"

"As you said, it's too much of a gamble to plead not guilty, so let's accept the DA's offer, go in there, and get it over with."

"Okay, I have a ton of documents to prepare. I'm going to the visitors' area, and I'll be back in thirty minutes to get you. We'll go to the court and get things rolling."

"I shore need a lawyer!" Cynthia said in a loud voice.

A guard opened the cell door, Amy walked out; then the cell door clanged shut. It was a sound imbedded in Kate's head especially now that she was on the wrong side of the cell. She walked to the bars separating her from Cynthia and said, "Cynthia."

Cynthia, who had been resting on her cot rolled over and said, "Yeah?"

"Cynthia, listen to me."

"I am. I am."

"I may not see you anymore, Cynthia."

"Wha? Where ya goin'?"

"I'm probably going to the Big House."

"Ya goin' where? Ya goin' to the Big House?"

"Yes."

"Ya can't leave me, Red! Ya can't leave me!"

"We'll meet again, Cynthia. I know we will and won't that be exciting…seeing each other again?"

"No! No!" Cynthia screamed; then she began sobbing. She scooted off the cot, stumbled to the bars where Kate stood, shoved her arms through the bars, and grabbed Kate. "No! No!" she screamed. "Them demons…they'll get me! They'll get me. Oh, no, no, no!"

Three guards walked hurriedly to Cynthia's cell. One unlocked the cell door, and the remaining two walked over to Cynthia, grabbed her shoulders, and pulled her away from the bars. Then one of them injected something in her arm with a needle.

"What are you doing?" Kate yelled. "What are you doing?"

Kate's cell opened, and Amy walked into the cell. "They're injecting her with a sedative," she said.

Kate looked at Amy. "Why? Why are they doing that?" she said, her voice loud. She could be heard throughout the cell block.

"They have to calm her down to prevent the entire cellblock from getting loud.

"I can't be with you any longer, Cynthia," Kate said, then turned to Amy. "What's our next step?"

We're going to make our plea. Are you ready?"

"Yes, I have all my belongings."

"Doesn't take long to pack a jumpsuit, does it?"

"Think heavy and travel light," Kate said.

"They're taking you in a van. I'll meet you there," Amy said.

Guards shackled Kate's legs, handcuffed her wrists, then guided her from her cell block and through the compound. Two sets of cell bars clanged behind them as they walked through the different areas. They exited the building, and the daylight shocked Kate's eyes for a moment. She was anxious to see the outside world, so she opened her eyes even though the bright light caused some discomfort. She looked from side to side to soak up every ounce of the view as possible before she would be forced into captivity. Being isolated and held prisoner had the potential of creating some digression in one's mental state, but Kate vowed that she would keep her mental state strong and that somehow, somewhere, something good would happen, and she would step out into the world and have more knowledge, strength, and grit than ever before.

The guards guided her to a sheriff's SUV, which was parked in an alleyway adjacent to the sheriff's office. One guard placed a ramp from the sidewalk to the rear area of the SUV.

"Get in and move to the middle," one guard said.

Kate walked slowly and carefully up the ramp. Then a guard forced her head down as she started into the back area of the vehicle. The seat was made of aluminum. Kate lowered herself onto it and scooted to the middle. Even though her buttocks were modestly healthy and full, the hard seat still caused her to wince. One guard entered to her left, and a second one entered from her right.

They arrived at the courthouse; the guards led Kate to the courtroom where she met Amy.

"We're first," Amy said.

Kate smiled.

The judge entered the courtroom, everyone stood, and the judge called Kate's case. "I need your brief, Counselor," the judge said.

Any stood and stated that the state had agreed to a plea of involuntary manslaughter and that was the plea.

Without hesitation, the judge accepted the plea, and then sentenced Kate to one to six years to be served at the Tennessee Prison for Women. She was escorted from the courtroom to the van that brought her to the courthouse earlier, and then driven to a holding area at the sheriff's headquarters. She remained there in complete isolation for five days without a hint as to when she would be transferred to the prison. On the morning of the sixth day, three guards appeared, and one advised her that they were taking her to a bigger hotel. One gave her a manila envelope with several documents inside and told her to present the package to the clerk at the hotel.

CHAPTER 15

It was a life-changing event as Kate rode the bus, referred to as the "Black Box," which had built-in shackles that were placed around the legs of each convict and locked. Kate estimated that there were forty women locked into the Black Box and she thought about what would happen if they were involved in a serious accident and the bus turned over. Surely, it would be deadly for all of the women.

She looked through the bars, which replaced the bus windows. Even though she couldn't determine the identity of the buildings because of the speed of the bus and the narrow space between the bars, she still knew they were going through the city and would soon be on the west side where the prison was situated.

Feeling the presence of all the women around her and knowing they were convicts, she reminded herself that she was one of them. She was conscious of the indignity as she sat among them and was well aware that all they were headed to a different life, perhaps a brutal life, and that they were leaving behind the civility they once enjoyed.

Only the engine of the Black Box could be heard. All the inhabitants of the vehicle were silent as they no doubt thought about losing their freedom and living their lives looking through bars and barbed wire. Two guards had seated themselves on the farthest seat in the back of the Black Box, and they occasionally walked the length of the vehicle.

Kate decided she would keep to herself, not make any friends, and use her time wisely so that she could be on the outgoing bus in one year.

The Tennessee Prison for Women spread ahead. The vast area was surrounded by a high chicken wire fence with razor wire formed in large coils along the top. Kate could see some buildings through the fence, but the area, for the most part, looked barren and desolate. It appeared to be shrouded in a gray cloud, even though the sun shined brightly on the cold November day. There was no noticeable life...no cars, no trucks, just a few concrete and metal blobs sitting on a huge patch of earth.

The Black Box pulled up to a guardhouse and stopped. All the passengers looked out at the guardhouse with all the curiosity that small children possess. The driver and the guardhouse attendant had a brief conversation; then a gate opened and the Black Box chugged forward to a second fence and another guardhouse. The attendant said something to the driver; then two uniformed guards bordered the vehicle, walked to the back, a gate opened, and the Black Box lumbered through.

"Ladies, the bus will be stopping at the corner of the building on my left. All of you will get off the bus and walk through the metal door with the black trim. Today is 'getting to know you' day. When you finish your 'check-in,' you'll be shown to your quarters."

One guard unshackled the passengers in the front row while two other guards stood nearby. As they were unshackled, they were ordered to disembark and go inside the building. They continued the process until they were at Kate's seat. In her head, she hated everything that was being done to her and certainly anything that she was forced to do. She hated the control that the guards employed, but she sat straight and looked straight ahead as the guards freed her from the shackles.

"Go through that door," a guard said, her voice stern and husky. She pointed toward the metal door near the corner of the building.

Kate stood up and retrieved the manila envelope that she had slid under her butt when she was shackled at the sheriff's office. It felt strange being free all of a sudden. Being free, then being shackled, then being free played with her head. She reaffirmed the promise to herself to be strong, so she stepped briskly to the front of the bus, down the steps, along a sidewalk for a distance of fifteen feet, then into a corridor of the building. A concrete floor, concrete block walls with no windows, and a guard seated at a desk flanked by three other guards welcomed her. She was officially a convict in prison.

"Your envelope?" the seated guard said.

"Yes, ma'am," Kate said, and then handed the envelope to the guard, who glanced at her with a quizzical look.

"What's your name?"

"Kate Patterson."

The guard looked at a sheet of paper fastened to a clipboard, and then glanced inside the envelope. She said, "Patterson, follow these two ladies. You're going to get a five-minute hot shower, and then we have a new outfit for you with your name embroidered on it."

"Yes, ma'am. Thank you," Kate said. She followed the guards into a concrete block enclosure with a shower.

"Take off the jumpsuit and get in the shower. You got five minutes. Exit out the other side," a guard said with an authoritarian tone in her voice.

Kate followed the guard's directions, showered hurriedly, took a towel from a shelf that held several towels, dried off, and walked into another concrete block room. She wore no clothes, but she did not worry about modesty at this point.

"Your new attire," a guard said, holding out a fabric uniform to Kate.

Kate took it from the guard and looked at it for a brief moment. It was a dull red jumpsuit with the name 'Patterson' sewed on just below her right shoulder blade. She put her legs into it, pulled it up, shoved her arms into the openings at the top, then zipped it up. She felt humiliated and helpless, but she reminded herself again that at the end of this day, she would have less than a year to go.

"Red means you're a badass" the guard said. "Means you get to sit out your time by yourself. Means you sit in your cell twenty-three hours a day."

Another guard said, "Patterson, you're going to see the doctor. Follow these two ladies."

Kate followed the two guards to a sealed-off area that had a sign hanging from the ceiling that read: Medical Examination. A suite of eight offices lined the corridor. She was ordered into the first office where a physical examination was administered. She gave a urine sample and a nurse drew blood. Kate believed the purpose was principal to determine if she carried the HIV virus. She then was ordered to another office where she answered a lengthy list of questions, some of them so personal that Kate had to remind herself again that she was in prison.

"Have you ever had sex with an animal?" a doctor asked.

"No, I have not," Kate said.

"Would you ever consider having sex with an animal?" the doctor asked.

"No, I would not."

"Do you suffer from anxiety?"

"No, I do not."

"Does anything in your daily living cause anxiety, for example, your work, your bills, your obligations?"

"Nothing in my life causes anxiety."

"If you were forcibly raped, what would you do?"

"As soon as I could arrange the means to kill the person, I would."

"You would not let the authorities handle the situation?"

"I would not."

"And why would you not?"

"Because the authorities, the courts, the justice system don't give a damn about my body. There are some things that happen to an individual that he or she has to solve by themselves. There are things other than death and taxes that one has to face alone and solve or handle alone."

"You know, that attitude will not go over well with the parole board."

"I could lie to you; I could give you a rosy answer. I could tell you what you want to hear. I choose to tell you the truth, and I think the truth will bear me out."

The doctor scratched the back of his head. "You have a point. I don't hear much of the truth in here," he said.

"That's sad."

"It is. I usually don't convey to my patients my evaluation of their psychological profile, but in this case, I'm going to make an exception. I don't understand why you're here, but you are. I don't see any of the usual tendencies in you that I see in other inmates. You are mature in your cognitive abilities; you have an uncanny grasp on the mechanics of life; you are blessed with your physical appearance. The warden is leaving in two weeks, but I intend to give a report to the new warden, and you will be named in that report. What was your occupation before coming here?"

"I owned a restaurant."

"So you're an expert restaurateur with a good knowledge of cooking?"

"I can hold my own."

"You'll be an expert in my report to the warden."

"I'm flattered," Kate said, then paused for a moment. "Or maybe I should be apprehensive."

"Oh, no, no! The report will be all good, and now your time is up. The guards are waiting for you."

"Thank you, Doctor."

"Let's take you to your new home," one of the guards said. They left the medical facility and began walking down the second-floor walkway.

"You and that room are going to get really acquainted," the guard said. "In fact, you're going to know every little speck on the wall and every little speck on the floor. Daylight is going to be like a miracle to you, but we're pulling for you and hope you're one strong bitch."

Kate listened but didn't reply. Sitting by herself may be a good thing, but it could be lonely. I'll take it day by day, she decided.

"You get an hour a day to exercise, make a ten-minute phone call, whatever you wanna do except mix with other inmates. Don't want you to rub off on the good people," the guard said. "You can have visitors two weeks from this weekend…Friday or Saturday only. Your visitors can stay for twenty minutes. Beginning with the third weekend after the present one, you can have visitors every week on Friday or Saturday for a total of thirty minutes. There will be no conjugal visits. Any questions?"

"No, ma'am."

"Leave the 'ma'am' off. You're not here to show your good manners. You're here because taxpayers don't want your ass out running around on the streets."

"I understand."

"Good!"

Kate followed the guard, a short stocky woman with very short hair, who walked in a slow, deliberate manner. Nothing except her legs moved when she walked. Her backend didn't move. It was like it was welded to the top part of her body. Kate took short, slow steps to keep pace with her. Another guard, armed with a billy stick, followed Kate.

They walked for five minutes passing doorways that resembled entrances to condos, on and on without any change—brown-looking walls, then a doorway; brown-looking walls, then a doorway.

The guard stopped, talked into a small microphone that was fastened to her shirt collar, keyed in something on a keypad, and a door opened. "Patterson, your new home. There is a bean slot here. When it opens, a tray will fold down on the outside of the wall, and your food will be placed on it. Any trash or any food that you don't eat will be placed on the tray within forty-five minutes for pickup. If you fail to meet the time for pickup, a team of pissed-off guards will enter your cell. If you cooperate with us in everything that goes on in here, we won't cause you any grief. If you don't cooperate, you'll be introduced to some pissed-off porcupines. Got it?"

"Yes."

"The bean slot is the only contact you're going to have with civilization until two weeks from this coming weekend. Enter your room."

Kate walked into the room, a space she judged to be ten feet by ten feet.

"That's your bed," the guard said, pointing to a small metal bed. "That's your sink and toilet. Here's your toiletries." She gave her a small fabric bag containing several items.

Kate looked at her new residence. The bed had a thin mattress and no pillows. The sink and toilet were metal, and the sink drained into the toilet, which was manufactured to form one unit. "Thank you," she said.

The door closed, and Kate was alone.

"I suppose they don't issue disinfectant," Kate said. She looked at a small indentation in the wall over the sink. "You are my new friend," she said, "and I'm naming you Mary. We're going to have a lot of conversations, you and me, over the next three hundred sixty-five days. Whoa! That sounds like a long time. What about saying a year? Which one sounds like the least amount of time? Well, when I wake up tomorrow morning, I'll have less than a year in here with you, Mary. Do you know it's four steps from my bed to the door? This is one small apartment.

"Here's another question for you. What do you think I should make my daily routine, that is, in addition to eating?"

"What? I didn't understand you. Oh, you said something? Okay, great idea! I'll rotate my day around eating. I'll exercise in the morning, have breakfast, take a little rest, then train my head to remember things to write in my journal when I get outta here. I'll have lunch, take a break, then exercise in the afternoon. When I get outta here, I should be one healthy bitch," she said, then laughed.

"Do you have any other ideas?" Kate asked, looking at her new friend, Mary. "No? What do you think I should do after dinner to make me sleepy and write off another day? Oh, you're right! I'll start on the left side of the wall, make a little prick…well, how can I remember the last prick from day to day? And, will the guards scold me for scratching on this rat hole? I'll just make it so small and insignificant that only you and I see it. I'll get plastic to eat for sure. When I do, I'll use a handle to make a very small scratch on the wall and work down, then back to the top and work down again. Each scratch will be a day. When I finish three hundred sixty-five scratches, I'll be outta here. I'll have to bid you goodbye, Mary. I'm sorry.

"Each time I finish one hundred, I'll put an X on the scratch and you and I will have a celebration. One day, I'll look up and see all the X's and say, 'Holy Crap'! There's an X, and there's another X, and there's a third X, and I'll say, 'Wow!'

"Well, you know, I have to be a real good inmate because I don't want to be here one day longer than my term.

"It's time…whoa! What is that? A cockroach! No! No! No! This is my house! You are not welcome," Kate said. She took off her shoe, bent down, and gently whacked it. She looked for its legs and selected one, used two fingers to carefully grasp it, then lifted it and threw it in the toilet.

"Mary, you can come out from hiding. I got it, and I flushed it. Yeah, I know. It's a terrible job. Okay, back to exercising."

Kate looked at the floor and decided against doing pushups. She believed the mattress was new, and if she could convince herself of that, she could do pushups in the bed. For now, though, she did stretches, curls with imaginative weights, standing toe touches, and arm-swinging exercises for what she believed to be forty-five minutes; then she sat on the edge of the bed and took a break. Several minutes passed; then suddenly the bean slot opened. Whoa! She could see out! She stood up and quickly walked to the opening. A guard placed a piece of paper and the ink holder of a ballpoint pen on the tray outside the slot.

"This is a telephone register," a voice said. "Write down the name, telephone numbers, and relationship to you of every person you're goin' to call or get calls from," the voice said. "I'll be back in one hour to get your paper and pen."

Kate took the paper and pen, walked back to the sink, which she used for a table, and said, "Mary, we have a job to do here. I have an hour to do it, so let's stretch it out as long as we can. Is that okay with you? Okay, good.

"Well, let's see. Mom will be first on the list, of course." Kate wrote her mother's name, home phone number, restaurant phone number, and "Mother" for relationship. "The café crew is next." She wrote Bobbie's, Sharon's, and Gill's cell phone numbers, the restaurant phone number, and "employee" for each as relationship.

"Mary, I don't want any of my customers to know I'm in the slammer, although it has probably been televised in every home and business in the country. The newspapers also probably got a kick out of my little escapade. For now, I think that's all the people I want to put on the list. Mom may have someone to add when I see her. I'll just call this a wrap. You know, that's something else I can do at night… think what I'm going to tell Mom. I need to think of a way to convey to her some keywords that'll cause me to remember what to write in my journal when I'm outta here."

She picked up the paper and pen and walked to the opening in the door, and then bent down and peeked out to see a handrail. Seeing nothing else, she placed the paper and pen on the shelf but continued to look out until a hand picked up the paper. She immediately pulled herself upright and turned her back to the opening so she wouldn't see the chute fall down, but she heard it and cringed.

"Mary, we're blacked out from the outside world again," she said. "It's about lunchtime, wouldn't you say?" Just as she finished the question, the chute opened again and a tray of food was placed on the shelf. Hurriedly, she walked to the door, picked up the tray, walked to her bed, and sat down.

"Mary, I would invite you to the table, but as you can see, we don't have one. Oh, I'm sorry. You want to know what we're having to eat. Well, let's see. We have a package of bologna…two slices, two small packages of salad dressing, two small mustards, three slices of bread, a small package of potato chips, a cup of tomato juice, a tiny red apple, and a…" she took a sip, "medium cup of Sprite. My, my, what will we have first? I sure don't like bologna, but hey, we're stuck in this little room with nowhere to go, so we'll just learn to eat it. I have a feeling we're going to see a lot of it.

"Mary, I hate to eat in front of you, but I'm hungry. I'm going to have two pieces of bologna between two pieces of bread with two mustards, a bag of chips, and a cup of tomato juice on the side. Gotta watch my figure, you know. Too bad, they don't serve lettuce and tomato. Wouldn't that be great? Just to taste a fresh tomato."

Kate ate the sandwich and chips, then drank the juice. When she finished with the chips, she wet the bag and wiped the toilet over and over until the bag fell apart; then she washed her hands twice.

She saved the third piece of bread, apple, and Sprite for an afternoon snack.

True to her schedule, she lay on the bed still in her jumpsuit, used her arms for a pillow, and took an hour's nap. When she awakened, she said, "Hi, Mary, I took a little nap, didn't I? All this activity sure wears me out. Okay, time to do some stretches. If I drag this out, it'll be dinner time, and I'll be that much closer to having this day behind me. I'll have less than a year to go.

"Mary, what part of the day or night do you think I get my one hour out of here? I mean I don't want to leave you alone, but it'll be a thrill to get out of my little apartment and maybe see other people even if they are convicts." Kate swung her arms from right to left, then left to right. "I hope it's not in the middle of the night when Mom's sleeping. I never dreamed of how confining and smothering it is when all your freedom's taken away."

The afternoon dragged on. Believing it to be midafternoon, Kate ate the apple with a piece of bread. She took small bites and chewed slowly so she could use as much time as possible. Between bites, she would sip the Sprite in a ritual manner because that, too, would chip away the time. She relaxed after her snack for what she believed to be half an hour, and then exercised again.

Finally, supper was delivered. It consisted of vegetable-stuffed cabbage, tomato sauce, parsley potatoes, mixed vegetables, two slices of bread, two small packages of margarine, a small apple, and a Sprite.

"My, my, my," Kate said. "We have a vegetable dinner! Our landlord doesn't want us to stay awake all night digesting a big, heavy steak dinner. They never thought about the fact that vegetables create gas. I may keep you up all night, Mary. If I do, I'm sorry."

Kate began eating slowly so as to consume as much time as possible. The mixed vegetables consisted of peas, whole kernel corn, and carrots. She ate them one at a time. When she finished, she believed she had used an hour to eat. Next, she sat on the edge of her bed and counted to one hundred. Then she counted again and again. After her third time, she did stretches and exercised for what she thought was an hour, and then brushed her teeth and lay down to sleep for the first night of her imprisonment. She found it very difficult to sleep for an extended period using her arms for a pillow.

After tossing all night, she awakened to see the small area of her confinement. She stepped into her sneakers, and then bent down and tied them. "Good morning, Mary. Sorry, I have to use the restroom without drawing the curtain. As you can see, there's no curtain. She went about her business, washed her hands twice, brushed her teeth, and then asked herself how she could do a body bath. She had no shower;

she had no towel; she didn't have enough soap, so she splashed under her arms, her chest, under her breasts, around the tops of her legs, and her thighs, and promised her feet that they would eventually get a shower. She did stretches, curls, and touched her toes thirty times, and then relaxed for thirty minutes until breakfast was delivered.

"Well, let's check this out. We have a small serving of oatmeal, a package of grape jelly, a package of margarine, two slices of bread, a very small orange, and a small cup of milk. Sorry, Mary, I don't have enough for you again. We're definitely going to have to get a message to the big guy and demand some food for both of us."

She ate slowly, placed the remnants of her breakfast on the tray, walked the four steps to the bean slot, returned to her bed, and sat down to take a break.

Thirty minutes passed, then suddenly the door to her cell opened.

"Patterson, you have an hour in the pub. You can use the phone for fifteen minutes. There are magazines and papers to read. There is a writing pen and there is paper. Whatever you write, you can have it mailed, or you can take it to your cell. Whatever you do, it must be reviewed first. Let's go. Here's your phone I.D. to call out," the guard said, then gave her an index card with numbers.

Kate was so excited she could barely move. She thought anxiously about freedom; she thought about calling her mother; she thought about writing and being able to bring the paper to the call. She became so excited that she couldn't decide what she really wanted to do, but she hurried out of her call to follow the guard along The Trail the down two flights of steps and finally into the pub, which was built in a hexagon shape. It spanned about fourteen feet by fifteen feet, Kate thought. She looked quickly from corner to corner, spotted the phone, the magazines, a writing desk with pen and paper, and a water fountain. She immediately walked to the fountain, turned on the water, bent down and sipped. It was cold and she allowed it to flow down her throat slowly. It calmed her whole being, but she raised up and quickly walked to the phone, picked it up, dialed in her I.D. number, then dialed her mother.

"Hello."

"Mother, Mother, it's your favorite daughter!" Kate said; then she heard a loud noise.

After a brief pause, a voice said, "Honey! Honey, it's you! It's you! How are you? Are you okay? Are they treating you okay?"

"Mother, I'm fine. It's just a little adjustment. I'm my mother's daughter, so you know I'm built of iron. How are things at the café?"

"They're fine, honey. Everyone wants to know where you are, of course. We're telling them you're in Europe at a culinary school."

"They didn't see me spread out on TV?

"Apparently not. When do I get to see you?"

"I'm confined to quarters for two weeks. I'll call you with the exact date and time. Speaking of time, I'm running out of it. So quickly, I'm really behind with my journal. When I see you, I want to give you some things to make notes so when I get out, I'll have the notes to catch up."

"Of course, dear. Must you go?"

"Yes, but I'll talk with you soon. Love you, Mother."

"My daughter, I love you."

"Goodbye."

For the next thirty-five minutes, Kate read magazines and wrote some thoughts down to take back to her cell.

CHAPTER 16

"Patterson."

"Yes."

"We moved a bunk bed into your room while you were out. You're going to have a roommate for a week or so," the stocky guard, who seemed to be assigned to Kate, said.

"I am?" Kate felt her body grow tense at the prospect of having a criminal housed with her. "Do you know who?"

"You get the luck of the draw. She'll be there about supper-time."

Kate's head reeled with so many questions. *How will they use the bathroom with some semblance of privacy? What if she's a gross ruffian and doesn't even care? What if she's mentally ill? Will I be able to close my eyes and feel safe? I can barely turn around in that coffin they call a room, so how are two people going to breathe in there?*

They walked for what seemed like an eternity, but finally, the guard stopped and opened Kate's cell. Feeling like a captured animal and knowing she had no recourse, Kate walked in. Neither she nor the guard said anything. The door closed, Kate was locked in, and the outside world was locked out.

She looked at the bunk beds, which had thin mattresses completely enclosed with tight, white sheets and had pillows with pillowcases. The upgrade in the sleeping accommodations was completely overlooked because of her apprehension about having a roommate.

"Mary, I'm beside myself. They're moving another inmate in with us. How are we going to exist? I mean, you and I can barely breathe. What are we going to do with another person?"

Kate sat on the edge of the bed and swung her arms from one side to another. It was a habit she had developed in the short time she had been locked up, but it helped her cope with the long minutes, hours, and days that she had endured since she stepped foot into the Nashville Prison for Women.

"What're we going to do? What're we going to do?" she said repeatedly. Finally, the afternoon passed, and the evening meal came. She thought about the guards calling it supper, but she called it dinner. It was a thought that took a minute or so out of the day and got her closer to getting her year over with.

She had seen the meal before because the same meal came on the same day every week. For tonight, it was chicken chow mein with chicken gravy, green beans, white rice, peas and carrots, three slices of bread, two packages of margarine, a small apple, and a Sprite.

"Mary..." she said but interrupted herself because her door suddenly opened.

"Patterson, your new roommate."

Kate stared at the woman and couldn't believe her eyes.

The new roommate held her head down and didn't seem aware of her surroundings.

Kate walked slowly to the new roommate, placed her hand softly on the woman's shoulder, and said, "Cynthia."

The woman raised her head causing her dirty blond hair to fall in tangles around her face just as it did back in the county jail. In very slow motion, her eyes seemed to walk their way up from the floor to finally look at Kate. She stared for a long time, then threw both arms around Kate's neck and shoulders and yelled so loudly that her voice reverberated off the walls and seemed to repeat itself. "Katie! Katie! Katie!"

Suddenly, a billy club crashed against the side of Cynthia's face causing her to scream with the resulting pain.

"One more sound out of you, and you'll get it on the other side," a guard said, her voice deep and husky, which was a perfect fit for her short stature and large chest cavity, which had the same circumference as the remainder of her body down to her legs.

Cynthia's legs began to collapse, and her body began to crumble as if it were an accordion. Kate grabbed her with both arms around the waist, but Cynthia was too heavy, and she slipped out of Kate's grasp and fell to the floor. Kate bent down and looked at the side of her head, which had immediately swollen with a huge lump with red and blue stripes.

"Miss, can we please get some ice and some sanitary pads?" Kate said, looking up at the guard.

The guard's facial expression did not change as she looked down at the two of them on the floor. Without any sensitivity, she walked out of the room, then the door closed and locked.

"Cynthia, Cynthia, I'm going to help you," Kate said. She put her arms under Cynthia's armpits and attempted to pull her toward the bed. "You're going on the bed one way or another." She grunted and pulled as hard as she could. Cynthia's body followed. Kate tugged again until they reached the bed; then she sat down on the bed still holding Cynthia by the armpits.

Kate looked around at the bottom bunk bed. "How do I get you up here?" she said, then tried to pull her up, but there was not enough room to scoot backward and pull her onto the bed. "What if I leave you propped up like this, then get down on the floor and lift you up? Yeah! That'll work!" Kate pulled her arms from beneath Cynthia and scooted around on the bed until she could get down onto the floor. She squatted and put her arms behind Cynthia's legs. She held them tight, drew them against her own body, and attempted to lift, but Cynthia's body didn't budge. "One more time," Kate said.

Suddenly, the cell door opened, and two guards walked into the room and straight to where Cynthia rested on the floor. In a joint effort, they lifted her onto the bed. They walked out of the cell, but one returned with a plastic bowl full of small cubes of ice, a small towel, and eight sanitary pads. She placed the items on the sink, and without saying a word, walked out of the cell. The door closed and locked.

"Well, well, it's as if they had a camera in here. Let's get to working on that head," Kate said. She dampened the towel, placed several cubes of ice on it, wrapped the towel so the ice wouldn't fall out, and placed it on Cynthia's head.

"Oh, oh," Cynthia said, her voice crackling with groaning sounds.

"We have to get that bump down, girl," Kate said as she held the wrapped ice to Cynthia's head. "You can't go to sleep until it's gone down quite a bit." After ten minutes, she wrung out the towel, rinsed it, and wrung it out again. She then filled it with ice and reapplied it to Cynthia's head. "Dinner's not too far off," Kate said. "Now, let's see. I know exactly what we're having. You wanna know?"

"Yeah," Cynthia mumbled.

"Okay, there'll be meatloaf with gravy, mashed potatoes, mixed vegetables, three slices of bread, two packages of margarine, a small orange, and a Sprite. Good eating, huh? The meat loaf's not worth a crap, but all in all, we're stuck where we are, and they don't have a Complaint Department here, so we can't complain, can we?"

Cynthia giggled in a deep tone that was barely audible. "Thank you," she said, her voice sounding low and strained.

"You're very welcome. I'm happy to see you, girl. I've been talking to the walls for four weeks, and they never talk back. It's been a little weird. No matter how much I tell them about what's going on, how I feel crappy, how much I would love to take a walk in the park and smell the grass and vegetation, they just never say anything. So like I said, I'm happy to see you. You've gotta get better because you're going on the top bunk as soon as you can. I'm afraid of heights, but don't you dare tell anyone."

Cynthia snickered and said, "Okay."

Kate applied the ice three more times, then said, "That bump's going down. Do you feel any better?"

"Headache," Cynthia said, her voice still sounding deep and barely audible.

"I'll see if we can get some Tylenol. This place is not like a hotel, you know. You can't pick up the phone and tell housekeeping you need something."

Cynthia snickered again, then rolled onto her back and looked at Kate. "That's a mean person that hit me and made my head hurt."

"I know," Kate said in a low voice. "Let's let you stay here on the bottom bed tonight, and I'll sleep on the top bunk."

"Okay."

"Cynthia, they brought you some pads, but there are only eight. You might start with two a day for two or three days and then cut back to one a day after that."

"Okay."

Kate climbed to the upper bunk and stretched out on the thin mattress. It seemed eerie looking at the ceiling so close to her head, so she turned on her side and looked down at the floor. That, too, was unsettling because the room was so small, yet the floor seemed very far away.

Forty-five minutes had passed when the bean slot opened and food was placed on the shelf. Kate climbed down, got the food, and they sat on the edge of Cynthia's bed and ate.

"This will be one story I have to record in my journal," Kate said in a low voice.

"Katie, when we get outta here, will you give me a job?"

Kate wasn't expecting the question, so she hesitated. "Will you be rid of the demons by then?"

"Yeah, yeah, they're goin' to send me to a program. They're gonna cleanse me of the demons. I really wanna work for ya. I'll do anything for ya."

"Well, then we'll just see what you're qualified to do when we're ready to get out."

"Oh, great! Oh! Oh! I can't wait!" Cynthia said, her face showing some natural color now.

The guards did an inmate count at nine o'clock, and the lights went out at ten.

"I'm sometimes afraid of the dark," Cynthia said in a low voice.

"You just tell the demons that I'm here," Kate said. "Whatever tries to keep you awake, we'll handle."

"I like ya a lot, Katie," Cynthia whispered.

"I'm glad you do," Kate said. "Why don't we try to go asleep?"

Cynthia became quiet, and Kate fell asleep. Two hours later, Cynthia yelled out. The noise startled Kate, and she jerked up not knowing where she was. "Wha...what's," she said, sounding as if she were in a stupor. As if stuck by a pin, she suddenly realized that Cynthia had cried out, and the guards would come bursting into the cell to shut her up. She jumped off the top bunk to the floor, then held her hands over Cynthia's mouth and whispered to her that she was there and everything was okay.

Cynthia mumbled something through Kate's fingers, but it was so dark that Kate couldn't see her own hands, much less Cynthia's face. Taking a chance, she decided to release the pressure on Cynthia's mouth.

"I'm sorry," Cynthia said, her voice barely audible and the words slurred.

"You had a bad dream?"

"Yeah."

"It's okay. I'm here with you."

"Will you sleep with me?"

"We both can't get in your bed, Cynthia, but I'll sit on the floor just where I am now, and I'll be with you all night."

"It's dark."

"I know it's dark. I'll lay my hand over yours so you'll know I'm here. There'll be no more demons tonight because if they try to come in, I'll grab 'em and body slam 'em to the floor of our cozy little house."

Cynthia giggled.

"Let's go to sleep."

"Okay, I'm glad you're here."

"Okay, go to sleep."

A few minutes passed and Kate heard Cynthia breathing deeply in measured intervals. "Thank god, you don't snore," Kate said, her voice barely a whisper. Several minutes passed, and she, too, fell asleep.

The next morning, Kate checked the bump on Cynthia's head and asked if she felt okay. "My head hurts a little, but I'll be okay. The lights are on."

"Yes, they are. Let's sit here a few minutes to wake up."

"I have to use the bathroom," Cynthia said.

"Go ahead. I'll turn my back, and when I go, you have to turn your back."

"Okay," Cynthia said, then wiggled out of the bed and stumbled to the toilet.

Later, they freshened up, had breakfast, and were talking about what they had just had for breakfast when the cell door opened.

"You two are getting an hour in the rec area," a guard said. "You'll be with other inmates. Any misconduct, while you're out, will land you in 'The Hole.' Be ready in ten minutes." The guard walked out of the cell, and the door slammed shut.

Kate's eyes grew big. "We're going out!" she said in a loud voice, and a glowing smile suddenly spread across her face.

"Oh! Oh! Oh!" Cynthia said, and then grabbed Kate's hands and forced her to go around and around in a circle creating a dance of sorts.

"Cynthia, Cynthia, what're we going to do when we get out? I know…as soon as we get out, let's take a real big breath of fresh air. After that, let's just stand and look at the sky. It doesn't matter if it's cloudy, sunny, or raining. Raining! Oh my god, what if it's raining? Won't that be great, Cynthia? Just stand in the rain and let it rain in our hair and down our faces," Kate said, her voice bubbly and filled with excitement. "Oh! Oh! It's almost time to go, Cynthia! We'll be gone a whole hour so use the restroom, and I'll step in the next room," Kate said, then climbed up to the top bunk and rolled onto her side to face the wall. When Cynthia had finished, she climbed down to the floor.

"Katie, we're gonna have a good time, ain't we?" Cynthia said, her voice upbeat. "And my head doesn't hurt no more."

"That's great, Cynthia!"

Just as Kate finished her sentence, the door opened, and a guard appeared. "Your hour begins now. Follow the other inmates to the rec area. When one hour passes, the tower will sound three bells. That means get back to your cells. You will not tarry. Do I make myself clear?"

"Yes," Kate said.

"Yeah," Cynthia said.

"Fall in line and follow the other inmates," the guard said, and then stepped to one side to allow Kate and Cynthia to walk through the door and onto The Trail. Five women were ahead of them, and six other women were behind them. One of the women who were behind them said, "Hey, Red, where'd ya get th' wig?"

Cynthia started to say something, but Kate elbowed her in the side, which caused Cynthia to look at her. Kate shook her head slightly back and forth indicating for Cynthia not to say anything.

"Yo, Red! The wig…where'd ya get th wig?"

Kate and Cynthia continued walking as if they had not heard anything.

Suddenly, the woman pushed forward, grabbed a handful of hair on the back of Kate's head, which caused her head to jerk backward in an awkward movement. "I said, where'd ya get th wig, Red?" The woman spoke in a loud, menacing tone.

Kate felt herself pushed aside; then a loud voice sounded. "Ahhh! Ahhh!" She righted herself and looked behind her to see Cynthia clinging to the woman like a wild animal. Her legs surrounded the woman around the waist as if she had jumped into the arms of the woman. Her hands held the woman's head in a death grip and viciously yanked it back and forth. She had plunged her teeth into the woman's face and was ripping the flesh from the woman's cheeks.

Suddenly, several guards charged into the melee, shoving, pushing, and then swinging billy clubs at Cynthia and the woman. Cynthia continued clawing at the woman's face, but under the barrage of blows from the billy clubs, she slumped to the floor. Meanwhile, another group of guards was beating the other woman.

Two guards grabbed Kate by the arms. "You're the instigator!" one of them said. "You're going to The Hole." Then the guards yanked Kate down The Trail.

CHAPTER 17

The bean slot opened, and a food tray was placed on the shelf; then the lights went on. Kate covered her eyes because the light played havoc with her eyesight. She had been in the dark for four hours, and the adjustment to light took practically all the allotted time for her lunch. She would be put back into the dark without eating all her lunch or any other meal.

When she could see without the pain and burning in her eyes, she told herself not to look around. She didn't want to validate the fact that she shared the Black Hole with mice and cockroaches. She had heard the mice squeak in the darkness, and she had felt them touch her arms.

She believed this was the beginning of Day 5, but the darkness twenty-four hours daily except for her meal periods confused her sleep habits. For many hours, she had only slept an hour or so. Whether she slept during the night or during the daytime, she couldn't determine. The darkness caused the daytime to be night and the nighttime to be night as well.

She stumbled toward the opening that held her food when suddenly the cell door opened, and two guards entered.

"Patterson, finish your food. You're getting a shower after you eat," a guard said. They walked out and locked the cell door.

The statement didn't create any excitement with Kate because her muscles were numb, her mind was numb, and any motivation she had once possessed had disappeared.

For once, she had been given a paper napkin. She used it to hold a piece of bread, then spread some meat-looking stuff on it and ate half of it. She ate half a banana, then drank some Sprite. Everything she ate was a chore; everything she did was a chore; every attempt to get her thoughts together failed.

Just as she finished, the cell door opened. A guard entered the room accompanied by a woman dressed in white. "Patterson, this is the nurse. She's gonna give you a vitamin shot. Two additional guards marched into the cell and positioned themselves on either side of Kate. The nurse lowered the bottom part of Kate's two-piece prison suit, wiped a spot on her buttock with an alcohol pad, and then gave her a shot.

"Patterson, these two ladies are taking you to get a shower."

Although she was not thinking clearly, something from her subconscious raised its head and caused her to say, "Hair?" with a barely audible voice.

"Yes, they are washing your hair."

One of the guards remained on Kate's right side and the second remained on her left side. They supported her as they led her out of the cell and to The Trail. They walked and walked, through several sets of security doors, past checkpoints, but finally arrived at a cleaning unit. They took off her two-piece suit, washed and rinsed her hair, soaped and rinsed her body, and then dried her. They dressed here in khaki pants, a shirt, and new shoes. After they finished dressing her, they led her to an adjoining room that had four patio-type plastic chairs and an accompanying table. Two women stood near the table each holding a container that resembled an overnight bag.

"Patterson, sit in this chair," a guard said, then pulled a chair from beneath the table for Kate. "This lady," a guard said, pointing to one of the two women, is going to work on your nails. While she does, this lady," she said, pointing to the second woman, "is going to work on your hair."

By now, the shot in the buttock was acting like an IV, and Kate was beginning to think clearly. She looked at her pants and shirt. They weren't prison attire. They were something you would put on to take a stroll in the park. As far as she could see, her name was not plastered anywhere on the shirt.

One of the women took Kate's hand and began filing her nails. The second woman took a position behind her and began brushing her hair.

Suddenly, a thought popped in Kate's head. 'I'm getting out here! Why? I don't know, but I'm getting out of here! Something's happened! My mother or someone else has pulled some strings, and I'm out! The exhilaration raced through her body like a wildfire leaping up a dry hillside. Her entire body tingled, which made her twitch. The woman working on her hands took a firmer grip on her hand. Kate smiled.

The process with her nails and hair was completed in an hour and ten minutes. As soon as the two women finished, a third woman appeared. She carried a case similar to the first two but carried a vinyl-clad footrest in her other hand and held a thick-looking pillow under her right arm.

"Scoot around, please," she said, motioning for Kate to move her chair away from the table.

Kate moved her chair away from the table and turned it so that she was sideways with the table and her feet stuck out with no obstruction.

The woman smiled and then placed the footrest next to Kate's feet. "Up, please," she said and scooted the footrest closer to Kate's feet.

Kate lifted her feet, and then the woman positioned the footrest under her feet, and placed a towel on it. "Down, please."

Kate complied, and the woman opened her case and placed several files on the towel. She then placed the pillow near the footrest, bent down so that her knees rested on it, picked up a file, took Kate's small toe, and began filing.

Forty-five minutes later, the woman finished, picked up her tools, and left. Kate looked down at her toes, which had been pedicured and painted with a clear polish to match the clear polish on her fingernails. She smiled. They were beautiful, and she would look spectacular when she walked out of the prison.

"Patterson, follow me," a guard said.

"Oh, my gosh!" Kate said, her voice in a whisper. "They're going to process me out!" Again, excitement and exhilaration raced through her body.

A few steps later, the guard stopped, opened a door, then stood stationary, waiting for Kate to catch up. "You're going to stay in here for a bit," the guard said. "Your lunch will be coming shortly. You have a bathroom, and please feel free to watch the TV. You have one hundred twenty-eight channels. The remote is beside it. There'll be a guard just outside the room. Go ahead in."

Kate walked slowly past the guard and entered the room.

"There are cosmetics and toiletries in the bathroom," the guard said before she shut the door.

Kate looked around the room and smiled. "I remember you," she said and pointed toward a side chair. "You're a chair, and I remember you too. You're a day bed, and you're a TV." She pointed at each one. "I remember you! I remember you! Okay, TV, what do I want to watch? News? No, no, I wouldn't know and don't wanna know what they're talking about. A good movie? Yeah! Yeah!"

She picked up the remote and turned on the TV. For a moment, it seemed strange to operate the TV and to remember what she used to watch. She scrolled through the channels and found a movie called *Finding Love at Christmas*. It was about a chance meeting of a couple who overcame one hurdle after another to get married. Tears came to her eyes as she watched the happy ending.

The door opened, and a woman came in carrying a tray. Kate quickly wiped the tears away from her eyes. The woman placed the tray on the table then left and closed the door.

"They're getting me fat and healthy before I leave this place," Kate said, smiling. She looked at the food, which was baked chicken, mashed potatoes, green, early peas, a half ear of corn, a fruit bowl, two dinner rolls, and cherry pie. The beverage was iced tea with two packages of sugar and two packages of artificial sweetener. She looked at the wall and said, "Mary, it's too bad you're not here to see the feast, and it's just in time because I'm getting a little weak again."

The sleep deprivation, food deprivation, and mental starvation had not magically vanished since she left the darkness in The Hole. When she had eaten only small portions of the food, she immediately rushed to the bathroom for a bowel movement. As she sat, she saw a bottle of laxative pills on the vanity, so they must have known that The Hole does horrible things to an individual.

She finished, washed her hands twice, and looked in the mirror. "Have you aged, my dear, or has this place just worn on you?" She looked at her hair and decided the hairdresser had done only a fair job; then she turned and looked at herself as much as she could in the mirror. Even in khakis, she thought that she still looked like a very desirable woman. She returned to the table and ate small portions of chicken and bread. She knew her kidneys had probably turned to a rock so she poured one package of sweetener in the tea and drank as much as she could. Seeing the pie, she couldn't resist, so she ate one bite. Still feeling weak and now feeling sleepy, she walked to the daybed, lay down, and instantly fell asleep.

Two hours passed, and the door opened.

"Patterson, wake up," a voice said, using a mild tone.

"Huh…wha?"

"Wake up. The warden wants to see you."

Despite her weak body and her deficient mental state, she recognized the word "warden" on the directory when the telephone rang. *She's letting me go. She's checking me out with a little sermon to take with me.* She looked around the room. "Goodbye, walls," she whispered.

"Why don't you freshen up a bit, use the bathroom, have a drink of tea," the woman said.

"Yes, thank you. I'll do all that," Kate said. "I don't want to keep the warden waiting though." Her excitement continued to build, and it was at a point that she couldn't decide what to do first. Adrenaline erased the trauma that her body had experienced, and she felt her heart beat rapidly, it too rising to the occasion.

She used the bathroom; then she washed her hands, brushed her teeth, gargled with mouthwash, brushed her hair, splashed water on her face, and dried it. "I'm ready," she said as she left the bathroom.

"We're not going far. The warden's office is just around the corner."

"Ready," Kate said and followed the woman. Her heart pounded now, and her chest felt a little tight.

"Here we are," the woman said.

They had entered a room that contained four desks, each occupied by a woman with their name embroidered on their right side above the bust area. Two guards stood outside the area.

"Kate Patterson to see the warden at his request," Kate's attendant said.

The woman behind the desk checked her computer; then she took Kate's thumbprint and checked it with the computer. She picked up the phone, dialed a number, and said, "Kate Patterson," and paused a moment, looked at Kate, and said, "Follow me."

Apprehension had now crept in replacing much of the excitement that prevailed just moments earlier, but Kate stepped quickly to comply with the woman's command. The door opened, and Kate walked into the office to see a modest desk with a chair turned backward so that she could not see the occupant.

Suddenly, the chair swiveled to reveal a man occupying it. "Kate Patterson, I'm Warden McNally. Have a seat."

Kate was stunned and confused. She knew very well that the warden was a woman, so her brain suddenly froze. She sat down on the chair, a burgundy leather side chair that looked more expensive than the warden's desk. She leaned forward, placed one hand inside the other, and extended her legs on the floor crossing them at the ankles.

"Ms. Patterson, this is Day 5 for me. Ms. Williams, who was the warden here for seventeen years, suddenly decided to retire. Not having another woman to take charge, the prison system assigned me here for ninety days. How are things going for you?"

Kate looked at the man, who was smallish in stature, perhaps five-foot-ten. He was balding at the crown, had several gray strands of hair, was hard-looking in the face, and resembled someone she had seen in a picture. "It's been a little tough, sir."

"So I've heard. I took time to look at your credentials, your past life, and it seems you had quite a regular life. You owned a restaurant, and everyone seemed to like you in the neighborhood."

"Yes, sir."

The warden looked at her as if he was reading every thought that was flying through her brain and also looking at her physical being as if he was seeing all of her through her clothing. "I'm in need of someone to help me with some particular duties. That person would not reside with the prison inmates; that person would be my personal aide; that person would reside in the room you just left. I'm here for a minimum of ninety days, so the person would be guaranteed some semblance of regular life and would then be that much closer to leaving this facility. The way the system works, I wouldn't be surprised if I'm not sitting right here one year from now. Would you be interested in being my personal aide, Ms. Patterson?"

Kate processed his rambling as quickly as possible believing all the time that he would want more than a personal aide, but she had a year to put behind her. She decided that she would handle things as they came. "Yes, sir, I would, and I'll be the best at whatever there is to do."

"Good!" he said, then rubbed one hand against the other. "I know your living conditions have been less than desirable, so I'm going to let you take the day off, let you rest, and we'll start tomorrow morning at seven sharp. A guard will escort you back and forth to this office. You'll have a cup of coffee on my desk at seven. I take one sugar and two creams. I like it very hot."

"Yes, sir. Do I get coffee from the mess hall?"

"Absolutely not! I have my own kitchen. It's that second door to my right. You will always prepare coffee there. You will always taste my food in front of me, whether it comes from my kitchen or if I order out.

"Your room has a pull-down bed. There is a clock radio in your room. You will set the alarm so that you can get a shower in the morning before you prepare my coffee. You will always be spotlessly clean when you report for work. I will let you go at six every night. You will have Sunday to do as you wish in your room. You may have visitors in your room for one hour on Sundays. The door will remain open with a guard stationed just outside when you have visitors. I am always out of my office on Sundays."

"Yes, sir."

"You will always refer to me as Warden. Any other name is forbidden."

"Yes, Warden."

"Do you have any questions for me?"

"No, Warden. You have been very concise. I will do a great job for you."

"That's all, Ms. Patterson. The guards will accompany you to your room." The warden then pressed a buzzer on his desk. The office door opened, and a guard marched in.

"Follow me," the guard said.

Kate walked behind the guard, waited until they were out of earshot of the warden, and said, "Are you going to be my daily guard?"

"I am."

"Good! I like that. You seem to be a pleasant person." Kate tried to see the guard's face to see if there was a reaction to her statement, but the guard looked straight ahead without speaking.

They arrived at Kate's room, and the guard opened the door. She said, "The door will be locked from the outside, and it will be unlocked at six-thirty every morning. You will have thirty minutes to walk to the warden's office, prepare his coffee, and have it on his desk promptly at seven every morning."

"What kind of coffeemaker is in the kitchen?"

"They have one that uses K-cups. You just turn it on and pour water through. Coffee and cream are in the cabinet behind the coffeemaker. The warden likes everything spic and span."

"I gathered."

"In you go. I'll see you tomorrow."

"Thank you. Good night." Kate walked into her room. "Quite a change from my past days," she said in a low voice. "I'll just watch TV." She turned on the TV but fell asleep immediately. Two hours later, the door opened, and her dinner was delivered. All food items and drink were on a tray, which she placed on the table. "My, my, things have changed. This looks like really good food."

She thought about Cynthia and decided she had to know if Cynthia had been injured with the beating she received or if she had just been thrown in The Hole. She would serve the warden well, jump at his every beckon call, and then ask him about Cynthia.

She ate only small portions of the food, then took paper cups of fresh fruit, white beans, a granola bar, and a piece of bread off the tray and placed them on the table with the intention of eating them later. Just as she did, the door opened, and a guard accompanied by another woman entered the room.

"We're going to give you another vitamin shot," the guard said.

"In the rear end?"

"Yes."

Without hesitation, Kate pulled her khakis down and bent over to touch the table. A sting followed.

"All done," the woman said.

"I'm glad about that," Kate said.

"You'll be sleepy in about forty-five minutes. Get all you want to eat, use the restroom, and do everything you do before you go to sleep," the woman said.

"In the past few days, I haven't had too much trouble getting ready for sleep," Kate said.

Without any response, the woman left the room, and the door locked.

For the next three days, Kate prepared the warden's coffee, prepared and served his lunch, received his dinner, which had been ordered from outside the prison, and she had tasted every portion of every meal. She decided she didn't have to eat her own food because by the time night came, she was full of the tastings of the day. On the evening of the third day, she gained enough nerve to ask the warden about Cynthia.

"What are the circumstances?" the warden said.

"Cynthia and I were allowed a break for an hour, and a woman began heckling me about my red hair. When she got no satisfaction, she jerked my hair. Cynthia is a friend, and being the tough person she is, she jumped to my defense and sort of tackled the heckler."

"So neither of you were at fault? That is...you said nothing to the other inmate... you or this Cynthia friend of yours did nothing to provoke the altercation?"

"That's correct, Warden."

"What disposition do you want of this Cynthia?"

"I would like her to occupy a room near me. I will keep her busy cleaning all the rooms on my block. She can also clean the walkways; she can collect laundry; she can disinfect all the doorknobs daily and any other object that different people touch or use."

"No way that I ever want her in this office or doing anything that concerns this office."

"Understood, Warden."

Two days later, Kate was told that Cynthia was in the prison infirmary. After two more days, she was brought to Kate's room at six o'clock in the morning. Her face and shoulders revealed extensive beating. Black and blue splotches covered the upper part of her body.

Kate attended to the warden's coffee at seven. After he consumed the coffee and asked her to prepare a second cup, Kate believed it was a good time to approach him. She said, "Will it be permissible for Cynthia to remain in her room for three days and to receive medical care during that period?"

"I will approve that," the warden said, and then opened his desk and removed a bottle. "I have here a ninety-day supply of birth control pills. Under no circumstances will you leave the bottle where an inmate or prison employee can see it. Under no circumstances will you tell anyone about the pills. You will take one in the morning every day. If you are uncomfortable with any concept of this, you can refuse to take the pills and return to the common prison population. Do you have any opposition to this?"

Kate knew this was coming, so it was not a shocker. She was in prison, and she had unwittingly been given the best position that any inmate could hope for. The prospect of returning to solitude and talking to Mary was compelling in making her decision. One could turn off their emotions, their thoughts, and their pride and respect for a few minutes, but one has no way to eliminate the mental deprivation of solitude. She would handle the situation the warden was planning one day at a time. She looked at him and even though she was thinking he was the lowest of all cockroaches on earth, she said, "No, Warden."

"Good! Then I will see you tomorrow morning."

A week passed. At the end of Day 7, the warden told Kate that he wanted her to go to her room, take a shower, and return to his office. The time had come, and she would rather be placed in The Hole for a day if given the chance, but as planned earlier, she would turn off her brain and endure the repulsive happenings.

During the next six weeks, except for Sunday, she met the warden nightly and pretended to respond physically while thinking of her mother's garden and how green it was during the spring and summer and how she used to watch the leaves drift from the gorgeous trees that graced her mother's backyard. After every session, the warden would go into another room, and Kate would return to her room.

At the end of the day of the sixth week, the warden asked Kate to remain in his office. "Follow me. We're going for a walk," he said, then opened a door on the opposite wall from the entrance. They continued down a hallway for about twenty feet, then the warden opened another door that led to a small balcony that overlooked a fenced rose garden that Kate judged to be fifteen feet by fifteen feet.

"I discovered this little piece of the earth after the former warden left. It must have been her little escape."

"It's nice," Kate said.

"But that's not why we came out here. We're here because there are no recorders, no hidden mics, no cameras, and no eavesdroppers.

"In my former life, I was assigned to the Secret Service located at the White House. I accompanied the President of the United States for three years all over the world, whenever he wanted. He regarded me as a friend, a friend who protected him from any and all danger. But then came the day when a nutcase jumped the South Lawn fence at the White House and ran up almost to the White House. The president accused me of not manning the South Wall checkpoint, when in reality one of the agents assigned to the checkpoint had fallen to the ground in pain with what turned out to be a kidney stone. Meanwhile, the second agent was attempting to administer first aid to the first agent.

"So I was assigned to the prison system. Everything I had done for the president was for naught. All the training and dedication were wiped away in one swift swoop. I have grown to hate him and want to somehow get revenge. Like a miracle, two events have occurred. First, you happened, and number two, I have just been invited to attend an event at the White House.

"During my spare time, I happened to dig into your background. I was quite intrigued that several of your friends just met their Waterloo. Your mother was quite an artist, also. So I want to propose a situation to you. All records of yourself and your mother will be destroyed and will never be possible to retrieve. Your remaining time here at this facility will be a cakewalk. I have a feeling that sex makes you uncomfortable, so that too will be discontinued. In exchange for all those considerations, you will assist in a very small measure to help me accomplish something."

Kate had remained focused and very attentive as the warden related his history at the White House and his disdain for the president. Being the individual she was and given the makeup of her genes, she was almost certain what the warden wanted to achieve at the White House. To pretend her innocence, she said, "And what is that, Warden?"

"I want you to help me destroy the president," he said without hesitation.

The answer verified Kate's assumption, and it pleased her that she could read his mind. "And how would you do that, Warden?"

"No, WE would do that. Your mother used a powder that mimics a heart attack and is almost impossible to detect...short of a blood check, of course, and even that evidence disappears in five minutes.

"The president has a long history of heart problems. If the president ingested the powder via his tea or coffee, he would in the minds of all around him including his doctors have died of a heart attack."

Still calm, Kate said, "And how would you get the powder inside the White House and through several levels of security?"

"There are two dozen pair of ladies shoes with two-inch hills in the personal storage area. By some strange coincidence, all the shoes have hollow heels...some with one hollow heel, some with two. The powder would be transported in a hollow heel."

"And be detected by a security machine," Kate said.

"No! No! I know the weakness of the machines. I worked with them. I attended meetings to discuss their drawbacks.

"Now, the powder would be encased in a very thin layer of lead and another soft material, which I cannot disclose. The machines would not be able to detect what is in the heel. In the very, very remote possibility that it was detected, we would have a copy of the requisition showing the shoes came from the storeroom of a prison. Get it, they came from a prison where you can get drugs, guns, switchblades, powder…got the picture? We could validate our innocence immediately.

"The White House already has copies of our fingerprints, which would secure our identity. We would then only have to walk through the metal detector."

"And how do you acquire the powder?"

"Your mother."

"I'm sure that my mother would refuse to do that."

"I believe we will be able to convince her."

"Who would administer the powder to the president?"

"After we clear security and have some privacy, you will exchange your shoes for a pair that I will have in my luggage."

"Won't that look strange…you having ladies shoes?"

"Not at all. I will have a case containing all the attire you wear to the event. After we clear the security, I will instruct our attendant to deliver the case to you. You will remove the packet and pass it to me before the event dinner. I'm sure we will reside at Blair House, so there will be ample opportunity to achieve our goal."

"And why would an inmate accompany the warden to the White House?"

"You are a trusted inmate with talent and education above the rest. You are accompanying the warden to observe and collect information that will be used by you to conduct educational classes for other inmates on proper conduct and protocol for special events—or any event—once the woman leaves the prison system. Your instruction will cause women to want to know how to act. You will be a bright star throughout the system.

"The instruction will be a mandatory attendance for all women before their release from the system. Better yet, they must have twenty-four hours of attendance, and they must be approved by you before they go before the parole board."

"Back to my mother."

"You and I will visit her tomorrow. The event is two weeks away, but we must get started immediately."

CHAPTER 18

Kate looked out of the SUV window as it was being driven from Ronald Reagan Washington National Airport, its runway just across the Potomac River from Washington D.C. The river was visible on the right side of the vehicle as they drove along George Washington Parkway. The grassy area between the parkway and the river had been manicured, and it seemed to glow as the sunshine touched down and concluded its journey from the sun. She remembered the story about George Washington throwing a coin across the Potomac, but there was no way he could have done that. The river was really wide, and Kate was surprised at how still the water was, yet it had to be moving.

The SUV exited off the parkway, and as it transitioned from the parkway to the 14th Street Bridge, the entire south side of the city became visible. Kate had studied the outlay of the city, the monuments, the location of different agencies, and the function of each one. The Pentagon became visible to their left; the Jefferson Monument was situated to the left on the opposite end of the bridge; The Bureau of Engraving and Printing was across the Tidal Basin from the Jefferson

Memorial, and it too was on the left side; the Washington Monument was a little farther and protruded above everything else.

"This is a magnificent city," the warden said.

"It is that," Kate said.

"As a reminder, the event is at eleven o'clock tomorrow morning. There's a subway from the Blair House to the White House." Warden McNally spoke in a low voice. "We should be at the pickup point at ten o'clock. We can't keep the president waiting. The event should take no longer than an hour. Then we're all ushered out to a dining room for lunch."

"Thank you for the information. Will we have breakfast before we go?"

"I believe breakfast should be at seven. We should certainly finish by eight. That will give us two hours to dress and get to the subway stop."

"That should be sufficient."

They proceeded along 14th Street, took a left at Constitution Avenue, then right on 17th Street to the Blair House, the president's guest house, located across from the White House but slightly west of it. They parked, and then four men dressed in dark suits, white shirts, and dark ties surrounded the vehicle. Kate assumed they were Secret Service agents. One of them opened the SUV door and said, "Welcome to the Blair House. Please proceed up the steps. You'll be met at the entrance door. Your bags will be delivered to your room."

The warden and Kate scooted out of the SUV and walked up the steps. Another man dressed like the first four met them and escorted them into the foyer, which was rather small and not as wide as in some grand residences. As they entered, Kate thought the décor was not only simple but also elegant. A grandfather clock was prominent; it stood at the opposite end of the foyer. A marble table with a scrolled Chippendale gold-clad mirror hung on the wall just above it.

They were immediately ushered into a room with security machines. They were told to remove their shoes and belts, empty their pockets, and walk through the latest in security: the Walk-Through, No-Touch Security Pat Down machine. Once inside the machine, which resembled the airport walk-through security machines but was bulkier, automated glass doors shut, and a robotic female voice said, "Air puffers on." Then high-pressure bursts of air were directed up and down on the body, tossing hair around, ruffling shirts and blouses, and blowing skirts to perform a full-body pat-down.

All bags, shoes, belts, and any other containers were placed on a conveyor belt where they were scanned by an attendant. Afterward, all valuables were collected, placed in individual containers, tagged, and placed in a safe. All other personal items were collected by their owner and put on to wear or put away.

Kate was escorted to a third-floor bedroom, which had twelve-foot ceilings. The walls were covered with a calming yellow wallpaper. Two windows were adorned with pink, green, and yellow drapes with matching waterfall valances. Canopy draperies reaching the ceiling flowed down to pink, green, and yellow tufted headboards of two queen-size beds that were perfectly made with matching coverlets. A small mahogany table, with two straight chairs covered with pink upholstery, was situated against the wall near one window and was a striking addition to the room.

The beauty of the room was breathtaking to Kate. She walked to the window and looked out to see the White House. The Blair House, the room, the scene outside the window created a great rush of emotion that flooded her entire being. She stood in grandeur, and the horror of prison life was a memory.

A knock on her door jarred her from her inspired dream world. She opened the door to a young woman dressed in a tailored gray business suit with a white blouse and tie. She was a petite brunette with a dazzling smile. Standing at the attention she said, "Dinner will be served in the Lee Dining Room at six o'clock. Would you like to attend?"

"It would be an honor. May I ask you a question?"

"Absolutely."

"Mr. McNally accompanied me earlier today, but when we cleared security, we were separated. Have you seen him, do you know which room he's in?"

"I'm sorry, Ms. Patterson. I don't know where he's located, but I'm sure he'll be at the dinner."

Failing to think of an alternative, she said, "Thank you."

"I'll be back at five-thirty to escort you. My name's Casey."

"Oh, thank you."

The door closed, and Kate decided to check out the bathroom. Suddenly, a thought whizzed through her head. She hadn't had a period for six weeks. The thought sickened her. Then one thought after another flashed through her head. Maybe the time in The Hole had disrupted her system. The warden had to be the father. She despised him. What if she had an abortion? How was she going to explain getting pregnant in a women's prison? She sat on the bed and stared straight ahead.

At three o'clock, a knock again sounded on the door. Kate opened it, and Casey appeared holding a case that Warden McNally had brought to the Blair House. "Hi, again. I believe your evening attire is in this case," Casey said. "Would you like to check it?"

Still preoccupied with thoughts of missing her period, Kate managed to say, "Oh, sure...sure." She took the case, placed it on the floor, and opened it. "Yes, yes, these are what I'm to wear for the dinner, and these are for the event presentation tomorrow."

"The facility has a shop to help with your hair...not a full-service shop but the personnel is great to help you with some fluff. Would you like to see them?"

"Yes, I would. Do I need an appointment?"

"No. What if I show up at your door at four o'clock to escort you to the shop?"

"That's great! Also, we're attending an event tomorrow. Would it be possible for them to provide a touchup about nine tomorrow morning?"

"Certainly. I will see you at four this afternoon and at nine tomorrow morning," Casey said.

"Great! See you then."

Kate closed the door and looked at the case again. She pulled out a red evening dress, placed it on the bed, and then went to the bathroom and took a shower. Everything was a blur now. The prospect of her being pregnant overshadowed the beauty of the room, overshadowed the fact that she was out of prison and enjoying an unimaginable taste of freedom, and overshadowed the dinner, the event, and rubbing elbows with the President of the United States.

Suddenly, she remembered the powder in the heel of her shoe. She dried herself quickly, put on an elegant white satin robe provided by the Blair House, and walked hurriedly to the case that Casey had brought. It was supposed to contain a small white envelope that she was to use to insert the powder and then pass it to the warden. She removed all the clothing and saw a pair of shoes identical to the ones she wore. There was no envelope! Did the warden forget? What now! She was really confused.

The ability to communicate with him was really impaired. With all the security and facility employees, it would be too risky to attempt to go to his room. Besides, she didn't even know where he was. Was it possible they pulled him aside for interrogation? Was she next? The situation was critical. If the powder was discovered in her possession, her one-year sentence would stretch to a lifetime behind bars. She would have a baby inside the prison.

This was critical, critical, critical! She couldn't think what to do. This was a situation she could not control, and it was new to her. As a last resort, she decided to continue with the afternoon plans and hopefully see the warden at dinner.

She resumed getting ready for dinner. At precisely four o'clock,

Casey appeared and escorted Kate to a second-floor beauty salon. One of the women on duty said, "Oh, I get to fix your hair!"

Another woman said, "Beautiful woman! Red hair!"

Kate smiled at each of them and said, "Thank you."

Fifty-five minutes later, Kate had been given a shampoo and style. "Now an even more beautiful woman," the hairdresser said.

Casey escorted Kate back to her room and reminded her that she would return at five-thirty; then she bade Kate goodbye until then.

Kate went into her room and walked to the window. So many unresolved things were piling up, but she had no control over two especially important matters. The plan with the powder had a definite flaw, and the possibility of her being pregnant was extremely upsetting. Continuing to look out the window, she could see heavy traffic to the west on Pennsylvania Avenue and no traffic to her left in front of the White House; apparently, the Secret Service had closed the street for security reasons.

"I have always been strong," she said. "These things will work themselves out, so I will go about my business." Despite her seemingly positive attitude, she was still anxious.

During the time until five-thirty, she again looked at every article in the case but found no envelope. Frustrated, she went to the bathroom, pulled out the tufted seat, looked into the mirror, and said, "Let's get made up." She applied a small amount of light brown eye shadow, then dark mascara, and a very light touch of blush.

At precisely five-thirty, a knock on the door sounded. Kate opened the door, and seeing it was Casey, she struck a pose.

"You look spectacular," Casey said.

"Thank you. You're most gracious."

"Shall we go?"

"Lead the way," Kate said, then closed the door and followed Casey.

"The green gown is beautiful, but you make it spectacular," Casey said.

"You're too much," Kate said. "Do you work here full-time?"

"No, I go to George Washington University full-time. This is a part-time gig."

"Let me guess. You're studying to be a public relations specialist."

Casey laughed. "Well, no. I'm studying pre-law. After that, I'll attend law school and then hopefully pass the bar. After that, I'll be an advisor to the President of the United States."

"Wow! You have everything planned down to the last minute."

Casey smiled, then her cheeks turned slightly pink.

They continued walking until they reached a stairway. "Is it okay if we walk down?" Casey asked.

"Of course."

"The dining room's at the bottom of the stairs. You'll continue into the dining room without me, but I'll be just outside and meet up with you when you finish."

"Don't you get to eat?" Kate said.

Casey smiled and said, "Later."

Another attendant took over after Casey walked away and directed Kate to her place at the table. Warden McNally was seated beside her.

"Good evening," he said. "We were separated, weren't we?"

"We were."

"A Blair House representative is going to introduce everyone and then give us a brief summary of the history of the dining room. Until then, do you need to wash your hands?"

Kate looked puzzled. She had washed just before she came.

"Yes, you do," the warden said. He held her chair as she stood; then held it slightly away from the table while she maneuvered away from the table. When they were out of earshot of the diners, he said, "They took the envelope or dropped it when they checked my luggage. You will have to continue alone. Are you up to it?"

Kate looked at him and wanted to ask him if this was his plan all along. She paused a moment, and then said, "I'm a big girl."

A smile crossed his face. "Good! Good! Let's get back to the dinner."

They returned just in time to listen to the dignitaries being introduced. The acting director of the Federal Bureau of Prisons sat at the head of the table. Other dignitaries included two men and one woman from the Department of Justice. Warden McNally introduced himself and Kate, referring to her as a trustee inmate who was gathering material for a prison education class.

The statement immediately cast a gigantic dark cloud over her attempt to enjoy the time away from the prison.

A Blair House representative introduced herself and stated that President Truman had used this very room for his cabinet meetings. Then she explained the origin of the porcelain and the English Georgian pine paneling. Kate listened to bits and pieces of the history of the room, but she had real difficulty staying focused.

The dinner was a four-course affair. When it was over, Kate breathed a sigh of relief, took a slice of pork loin, a chicken breast, and two pieces of bread, wrapped them in a napkin, and then met Casey. "I brought this for you, just in case you're missing your dinner."

"Oh, how sweet! You're so thoughtful."

Kate smiled.

They returned to Kate's room, and Casey said, "Good night."

Kate went inside, changed into tan slacks and a green blouse. At nine o'clock, she opened her door and walked out into the corridor.

"Miss, may I help you?" a security officer said.

"I want to see the president. He's in grave danger."

"What kind of danger, Miss?"

"Sir, I realize you have to do your job, but this is for the president's ears only. Now, please call your superior and tell that person I must see the president now. It is of the utmost importance. It's a matter of life or death."

The officer regarded Kate with a quizzical look, apparently trying to decide if he should disturb his superior. "Just a moment, Miss." Turning sideways, he spoke into a microphone, which was attached to his coat collar. His facial expressions changed several times before saying, "Follow me, Miss."

Kate followed the officer to the first floor of the building; then they walked to a small office. "You will see Major Billings."

"Thank you," Kate said and walked into the office.

"I'm Major Billings. What seems to be the problem?"

Kate looked at the major, a distinguished-looking man with thin gray hair who stood only a few inches above herself and was deathly pale. "Major, I have an urgent message for the president. It is not for you to hear; it is not for your superior to hear; it is not up for discussion. It is a message that I must give to the president and him alone. If I am denied a meeting with him, and if something dreadful happens to him, then I will call a television network and tell them that your office denied me permission to warn the president of the grave danger he was in."

The major looked at Kate in the same manner as the first officer, then dismissed himself apparently to make a phone call. Two minutes later, he returned. "Follow me. You must go through security."

Kate followed the major to the room with security scanners where she was again scanned and patted down, then released to the major.

"Follow me," he said. They took an elevator to a lower level and walked to an area with small cars that resembled miniature subway cars. "Step aboard," he said.

Kate stepped into a car followed by the major; then an electric hum sounded, and they were in motion. Only a few seconds passed, and the car stopped.

"Follow me," the major said.

They walked to an elevator, stepped in, and the major pushed a button. They ascended for twenty seconds and stopped. "Follow me," he said. They walked through a non-descript corridor for a brief time; then the major stopped in front of a solid door. Two men dressed in dark suits approached them and stopped. Two other men appeared at the end of the corridor and remained in that position. One of the men who were near them opened the door and said, "Please take a seat."

Kate and the major entered the room, a small office with a desk, two side chairs, and two wooden chairs with arms and padded seats situated in front of the desk.

There was complete silence in the office and outside the office for five minutes; then one of the men outside the office door asked the major to step into the hallway. Two men in suits entered the office, and then a third man followed.

"Miss, I am the president. These gentlemen are with the Secret Service. They must remain. What is your name?"

"Kate Patterson. I apologize for interrupting your night, sir, but what I have to tell you is extremely important to your well-being."

"Please explain."

"Do you recall Adam McNally, who used to be with the Secret Service?"

"I do."

"Mr. McNally, as you know, is now a warden presently at the Women's Prison in Nashville. He wants to do you harm, and he enlisted me to help against my will."

"And when is this incident supposed to happen?"

"Tomorrow at the luncheon."

"Is it Miss Patterson?"

"Yes, sir."

"Miss Patterson, are you one hundred percent reliable? Can I trust you?"

"One hundred percent, sir."

"What if I were to ask you if you could handle the situation, Miss Patterson?"

"I would say to you, sir, absolutely."

"Then this meeting is over. Do you have anything else?"

"No, sir."

One of the men stepped out into the hall; then the major came to the door and said, "Follow me. Good evening, Mr. President."

They returned to the Blair House, and Kate was escorted to her room to find Casey waiting for her.

"Hi! Since you're getting your hair done tomorrow morning, we've rearranged your schedule. Wake-up call will be at six-thirty, breakfast in the Lee Dining Room at seven-thirty, hair at nine, and depart Blair House at ten-thirty. You'll have about forty-five minutes to change clothes after you get your hair done, so you'll want to do as much preparation as you can before breakfast. Have I really mixed you up?"

Kate laughed. "No, you've been perfect. Besides, you'll be with me every step of the way, so I can just relax and let you guide me to the next event."

Casey laughed. "That's the spirit! May I get you a drink or maybe a snack?"

"I would love to have a glass of unsweet tea with a lemon and a pack of peanut butter crackers."

"Now, that's a challenge," Casey said and laughed. "I'll be back in ten minutes."

Kate smiled, then went into her room and left the door cracked. Sure enough, Casey was back in ten minutes.

"Tea and crackers. Anything else tonight?" Casey said.

"No, thank you. You're a jewel. I'll see you at seven-thirty," Kate said and then shut the door. She ate the cookies and took the tea to the bathroom. She showered, sipped on the tea, brushed her teeth, applied a night cream provided by the Blair House, and then thought about the next day. She would have to improvise once she got to the luncheon. The powder certainly couldn't go in a glass or in any other object that would have a residue. She was dealing with the Feds now, so there was no margin whatsoever for an error.

She checked the time on the elegant gold clock in her bathroom and said, "Oh, my gosh! It's eleven-thirty! Bedtime!" She changed into her gown and crawled into bed and turned off the lamp.

The next morning, she awakened and the lack of sleep affected her usual energetic outlook of the day. "I'll perk up with breakfast," she said. She took inventory of all the items she would wear to the luncheon. Warden McNally had even packed a small evening clutch purse, which Kate debated about taking but decided she would.

The morning went as planned, and it seemed as if by the twitch of her nose, she was standing at the subway car that she had ridden the night before. This time, Casey accompanied her. Warden McNally was nowhere to be seen, but once at the White House and being guided to the luncheon dining area, the White House personnel had them seated side by side and at the farthest end of the table. The speakers would be at the opposite end and would cause everyone to look their way and away from where Kate and the warden were seated.

"Good morning," Warden McNally said. "How's the day going for you?"

"Everything's fine, sir."

"No complications with sleeping or your room?"

"No, everything's fine."

"The president is supposed to be here soon, and I believe we begin eating after he arrives. By the way, do you like cherry tomatoes?"

"I can take them or leave them."

"Cherry tomatoes are my favorite fruit and also the favorite of the president. He would always have a bag when we flew around the country."

Someone started speaking from the opposite end of the table, and Kate took the opportunity to take a small vegetable knife and drop it in her purse. Then she quickly dropped a cherry tomato into the purse. She touched Warden McNally on the arm and said, "I'll be back in a minute." She scooted her chair back quietly and then tiptoed to an attendant stationed near the table. "Will you direct me to the ladies room, please?"

"Certainly, follow me."

The attendant guided her to the ladies room and said she would wait for her.

Kate walked inside, and then opened a stall door, went in, and locked it. As if the architects knew the importance of a shelf, they had attached one to the wall inside the stall. Kate placed her purse on the shelf, took out the knife and cherry tomato, and carefully cut a circular cone where the stem had been attached to the tomato. She placed a piece of toilet paper on the shelf, and then put the knife, the tomato, and the tomato cone on the paper. She sat on the toilet and hurriedly took off her shoe, forced the heel upward, and twisted it until it separated from the shoe.

The package was very small and had a tit on one end that she twisted off and dropped in the toilet. Next, she carefully emptied the contents of the package into the opening of the tomato and watched as the powder dissolved into the tomato. She dropped the package in the toilet and flushed it. She slowly placed the cone into the tomato, put the knife back into her purse, and then placed the tomato in a small pocket of the purse so that it would not turn over.

She checked the toilet, replaced the heel of the shoe, put it on, and left the stall. She washed her hands thoroughly twice. The entire exercise took just a little over two minutes. She walked out of the ladies room and didn't notice a man walking toward her.

"Miss Patterson."

The sound startled her and she jerked quickly to look at the person calling her name. "Mr. President."

"How are you, Miss Patterson?"

"I'm fine, Mr. President. I was daydreaming, and the sound of my name startled me for a moment."

"Is there anything I can do for you?"

"No, sir, I appreciate your interest. I'm fine. Thank you."

The president walked away and Kate returned to the table, sat down, and said, "I just saw the president."

Warden McNally's eyes grew big, and a smile flashed across his face. "You did? Did everything go okay?"

"Like a charm."

He smiled and rubbed his hands under the table.

"The President of the United States. Will everyone stand, please."

As chairs were being pushed back making noises, and while everyone was moving to stand, Kate slipped the knife back onto the table and exchanged the cherry tomato for one that was centered on top of Warden McNally's salad.

After a speech by the president, everyone was invited to eat. Kate picked at her salad while Warden McNally ate with much enthusiasm.

Someone at the opposite end of the table rose and proposed a toast to the president. Everyone stood, then suddenly Warden McNally grabbed his chest. He quivered for a moment, then fell forward with a thud on the table.

"Someone call a doctor! He's having a heart attack!" Kate said loudly.

Three men, one with a stethoscope, ran quickly to the warden and listened to his heart. Almost immediately, all three men lifted the warden and carried him away.

For the next hour, there was chaos as the attendees gasped at the horror they had witnessed. The dinner and event were canceled, and Casey escorted Kate back to the Blair House.

Later that day, Casey accompanied Kate to a snack bar, and they ate a sandwich. The day ended without any communication about the event.

The next day was also void of any communication. Casey joined Kate for breakfast and lunch, but that was the extent of any interaction with anyone.

At four o'clock in the afternoon, two men dressed in suits appeared at Kate's door.

"May we come in please?" one asked.

Kate stepped back, apprehensive. "Sure, come in," she said.

Miss Patterson, you are being returned to Nashville tomorrow at noon. An escort will come to your room at that time and accompany you for the trip. You are being assigned to a halfway house for a period of two weeks; then the president will pardon you. Your friend, Cynthia, will also be pardoned. There is a stipulation, however. You will employ her for a period of one year. You will see to it that she remains drug-free, and you will see to it that she undertakes elementary training at a qualified institution to provide her with a jump start on everyday living. Are there any questions?"

Kate looked at the men. She was dumbstruck, she couldn't speak. She walked to the writing desk, pulled out a piece of paper, and wrote in the largest possible letters for the page...THANK YOU, MR. PRESIDENT!!!

"Please give that to him," she managed to say.

EPILOGUE

"What a wonderful birthday party," Kate said. "You are five years old now and don't let the teasing about your red hair bother you. You are unique. You're one of a kind, a beautiful girl who Granny Sara and I love very much. Now that everyone is gone, Granny Sara and I want to talk to you about when you grow up and what you have to do to take care of yourself."

"Okay, Mommy."

ABOUT THE AUTHOR

Bryce literally grew up on a mountaintop in East Tennessee. A dirt road ran in front of his family's home just twenty feet away. During the summertime when an occasional car passed, a dust storm delivered a fresh layer of dirt that was deposited on all the grass and the front part of the home, including the windows and the porch.

When he wasn't in school, he wandered alone along trails through the woods where he majored in one of the courses that Mother Nature offers . . . imagination. Rays of sunlight that slipped through the canopy of tree leaves and skipped along the trail became lighted, livable objects; a rustle in the underbrush became a giant monster that was attempting to escape from the brush; a whistle from a bird became an invitation for him to follow it to a magical part of the woods.

He often got into trouble with his grandfather, who owned a barn with a hayloft full of hay. He and his buddies would use the hayloft for a wrestling venue. Bundles of hay would be broken and then scattered about the hayloft. When his grandfather would discover the mess, he would come looking for Bryce.

When Bryce thinks about his young life on the mountaintop, he thinks of himself as just another Hucklebery Finn.